Precarious Balance

A Novel by

Rosemary Townsend

Order this book online at www.trafford.com
or email orders@trafford.com

Most Trafford titles are also available at major online book retailers.

Cover: *Goldfish* by Henri Matisse
Permission to use the image granted by the Heirs of Matisse
is hereby acknowledged with gratitude.

Printed in the United States of America.

ISBN: 978-1-4669-9421-8 (sc)
ISBN: 978-1-4669-9423-2 (hc)
ISBN: 978-1-4669-9422-5 (e)

Library of Congress Control Number: 2013908498

Trafford rev. 06/07/2013

Trafford
PUBLISHING· www.trafford.com

North America & international
toll-free: 1 888 232 4444 (USA & Canada)
phone: 250 383 6864 ♦ fax: 812 355 4082

*Dedicated to
my husband
Roy*

Contents

Summer

i thank You God for most this amazing
day: for the leaping greenly spirits of trees
and a blue true dream of sky; and for everything
which is natural which is infinite which is yes

(i who have died am alive again today,
and this is the sun's birthday; this is the birth
day of life and of love and wings: and of the gay
great happening illimitably earth)

how should tasting touching hearing seeing
breathing any—lifted from the no
of all nothing—human merely being
doubt unimaginable You?

(now the ears of my ears awake and
now the eyes of my eyes are opened)

(e.e. cummings, 1894-1962)

December

The oak leaves are out in full, becoming a darker green than before. Turning fifty is behind me, Lord, and it all went better than anticipated. It is a good age to be, after all.

Help me, Lord, to become older gracefully. Grant me courage, grant me peace.

With that, Clare closed her journal, and said to herself, All else can wait.

Clare was watching the goldfish in the pond at the bottom of the garden. She had taken an early morning walk to do so. This was where she sometimes came to think things through, and this morning was such a time. There was a still freshness in the air that flushed her cheeks and helped her towards clarity of mind. She was deeply concerned and needed to gain perspective.

There were often tricky situations pertaining to family, friends or acquaintances that she felt needed her prayers and love. Discovering how she could be a possible part of the solution needed reflection. The shady nook in her garden was an ideal place for this. As her two sons grew and developed into adults, their needs naturally changed, and she had to make sure she was not stifling them with her habitual maternal instincts.

Her younger son Matthew, aged twenty-three, was in love with a young woman, Nicole Hayden, who Clare had reason to believe was seriously ill. When she recently saw Nicole she had an almost deathly pallor. Nicole's doctor had scheduled her for an appointment with a haemotologist later that day. Clare had asked Matthew to let her know the outcome at the earliest opportunity.

'I will, Mum, as soon as we know. In the meantime, keep her in your prayers.'

And Clare was doing just that. For her not to pray would be like ceasing to breathe. It was her life force, her central focus, her reaching out to her Beloved. Her husband, Craig, understood this, although he did not share her ardour.

Craig MacMillan was already in his study working. An economist of note, and a consultant, he studied the financial world to keep abreast of current trends. The past year had been particularly stressful due to the onset of the financial crisis in the United States and the instability in the South African market caused by the abrupt recalling of its president. There were a number of younger people he mentored, regarding their offshore investments, some of them friends of his sons. They came to see him in his home office, and so Clare also got to know them.

Clare and Craig had settled into a comfortable pattern where there was still space for passion but where the relationship was not dependent on it to move forward. When she was twenty, Clare had been desperately in love with a suave and wealthy lawyer, who whisked her around the world in luxury ocean liners and private jets, but passion had at last consumed the very relationship itself. When Craig came along he was so solid, so reliable, so stable and so homely by contrast that she gravitated towards him like a rose to gentle rain. So from the start Craig enveloped Clare with a sense of security which felt like the warm, loving embrace of a friend rather than the passionate kiss of a lover. Not that there wasn't room for both.

Clare mostly felt very grateful for all her blessings. Sometimes, though, when her elder son Jerome and Craig were more grumpy than usual—or when her gentle Matthew was uncharacteristically sharp—she longed to return to the harmonious rhythm she normally enjoyed.

Later in the day, when she was busy sculpting in her studio, making a bust for one of her clients, Matthew called Clare.

'Mum, start praying with even greater seriousness. Nicole is very ill. I'll tell you more when I get home.' Matthew still lived partially at home, but mostly in the apartment he was busy renovating.

'It's a kind of cancer, Mum,' he said, before he'd properly entered the kitchen. 'A kind of leukemia. They've caught it relatively early so there's hope, though to Nicole it feels like a death sentence. Please pray for her, Mum.'

By now Matthew was sitting down at the kitchen table, his head in his hands, trembling, distraught, and trying to talk hope into himself. They had thought Nicole might be anoerexic, as she'd been off her food and lost a lot of weight suddenly. That seemed bad enough but this seemed worse.

'What is the prognosis, darling? What did the haemotologist say?'

'He said Nicole must start on a course of chemotherapy immediately and if she responded well, there was plenty of reason to be hopeful. Mum, we have to pray with all our might that she will respond positively to treatment.'

'Of course I shall join you in praying with all my might for a successful outcome. For Nicole's sake, we must all express full confidence and hope. Our faith will be stretched but God always rewards faith in him. His goodness will prevail over evil.'

'Will it, Mum? Can you be sure? That is what I want to believe too. Thank goodness Nicole's parents are also Christians, particularly her mum is being very supportive through all of this. Please reach out to her at this time, Mum. I'm sure she'll need a friend like you.'

'I will, darling, if you think that will help.'

'You're a star, Mum, and you're able to inspire people. Nicole's whole family will need all the help and inspiration they can get.'

By now Matthew had a piping hot cup of tea in his hand and his trembling had ceased. He had transferred his burden onto his mother as so often during his childhood when he was troubled or alone. He simply knew things would improve now that she had taken on his load. He felt free to love and support Nicole and to leave the earnest intercessory stuff to his mother. Her prayers would pull them all through. He had more faith in her faith than in his own, but ultimately he knew that they all worshipped and trusted in the same God, who would come through for them. Now it remained for him to persuade Nicole of this.

'May I have supper as soon as possible, Mum? I still want to pop out briefly to see Nicole before she goes to bed.'

'Of course, darling, and give her our love and assure her of our prayers. Have you told Jerome?'

'No, could you please do that? You'll do a better job of it.'

Before long he was gone.

Clare picked up the phone to contact her elder son. Jerome was studying medicine at the University of Cape Town. A karate instructor, he was emotionally more independent from his parents than Matthew. Jerome had lived in his own apartment for some years and, while studying, worked for a gym club over weekends where he instructed students aged four to seventy in the basics of karate. He had become a karate master himself some years previously.

Among Jerome's students was a boy of thirteen, who showed great promise. Luca Romano came to karate classes twice a week, on a Thursday afternoon and a Saturday morning. Jerome liked the intensity this young man brought to his martial art, and he sensed in him also a particular affinity. Luca was always the first to arrive and the last to leave. In addition, Jerome noticed he tended to linger after class to exchange pleasantries with him. He seemed focused on his sensei in a way that was both endearing and somewhat perplexing. Jerome would discover the reason why much later. For now, he humoured his pupil by making light conversation. Mostly Luca wanted to know more about the background to karate and why certain moves were more powerful than others, the reason behind the different positions, and the origins of the art. In class Jerome focused on the physical aspect of the sport and few pupils were interested in the philosophical underpinnings, so he too enjoyed his talks with Luca.

'Nice class, sensei,' Luca said one evening.

'Thanks, Luca. I notice you've been doing a lot of practising at home.'

'Yes, sensei. It helps me when I'm upset to think straight.'

'Are you often upset?' asked Jerome, picking up on his cue.

'Sometimes. My parents are divorced.'

'Oh, I'm sorry to hear that, Luca.'

'It's okay, sensei. It's better that way . . .'

'But it's still difficult, Luca, I'm sure.'

'Yes, it is, sensei.'

After this conversation Jerome was more aware of Luca in his class and ready to offer an encouraging word.

At the last lesson before Christmas, Luca asked Jerome if he would mind giving him his personal mobile number. Jerome normally worked through the receptionist at the training centre where the classes were held. But there was something in the urgency of his pupil's voice which made Jerome relent and give it to him.

'This is for your personal use only, Luca,' he said. 'Please do not pass it on to any of your fellow students.'

'And I'll try not to use it, sensei. I'll do my best not to use it. In case of emergency only.'

'That sounds serious, Luca. Is there anything you want to tell me?'

'Maybe next year, sensei. Nothing for now. Have a happy Christmas. I'll practise my karate at home.'

'I know you will, Luca. You are my most dedicated student. I wish you and your family a good Christmas too.'

This last conversation with his student haunted Jerome over the Christmas period but he didn't want to get too involved. He decided to use his mother's method and hold up this young man in prayer. He might even enlist her help to do the same.

So when they did speak on the phone, Clare told him about Nicole and he told her about Luca. They promised mutual support, each strengthened and reassured by the other.

The lush neighbourhood of Constantia where Clare and Craig lived contained gems of tradition and stately beauty like Groot Constantia with its gracious homestead and vineyards and Schoenstatt convent with its exquisite grounds and shrine.

Nevertheless, despite its idyllic nature, the outside entrance to most Constantia homes had the typical South African feature of most wealthy suburbia and was governed by a remote which opened the security gate leading into the driveway. Craig and Clare's home was no exception.

So on the mornings when their domestic helper Elsa arrived, Clare opened the gate for her from inside the house. Elsa had her routine, and there was normally a companionable silence that reigned between her and her employers. Craig and Elsa greeted, and that was about it. But Clare kept abreast of developments in Elsa's family, particularly with regard to her two children, who were both in a good primary school in the nearby suburb of Retreat, funded by the MacMillans. Clare had learnt over the years that becoming too close to Elsa's world and its problems made the relationship a stressful one rather than a helpful one to her. Its primary purpose was then undermined, although its secondary purpose for Clare was indeed to facilitate her outreach into the local community Elsa represented. Together she and Elsa hosted an annual Christmas party for Elsa's children, their cousins and their friends. This took place in the school hall and provided great mirth. Elsa and Clare went shopping in advance to get suitable Christmas presents. This year they were having the party on Saturday, the 13th of December, before the frenzy of Christmas fully set in.

'It is good of you to do this, Clare. I say this every year, I know, but it truly is good of you to do this.' Craig spoke in a tone full of admiration and appreciation.

'I only hope I am not being condescending.'

'No, you are not. Elsa knows you. You never condescend to her. Why would throwing an annual Christmas party for children be construed as condescending? You have too many scruples.'

'Thank you, darling, for reassuring me. I think I simply need to do this in the best faith I can muster and not allow myself to be overly self-conscious. This country has certainly inhibited our naturally generous impulses, hasn't it?'

'Yes, it certainly has, so resist it with all your might. You go and enjoy it all, sweetheart, just as you always do, and focus on the good time the kids are having. They don't care about condescension, they only care about the fun you are encouraging them to have. And Elsa greatly appreciates it, you know she does.'

'Yes, I do know, you're right. So I'm going to go out there and have a fine time myself. It always reminds me of the great parties we used to have for our boys. Do you remember how tremendously sociable Jerome was as a ten-year-old, and even as a thirteen-year-old? Some of his parties were exhausting but oh, such fun! He only became a bit withdrawn at the age of about sixteen.'

'Don't worry about that now, Clare.' Craig sounded somewhat stern. 'Focus on enjoying yourself with Elsa and the kids today. I want a good report when you get back.'

And he got one. The party was a success.

The children were naturally boisterous, and the cool-drinks, cake, and sweets made them more so, but Elsa and Clare were rewarded by the laughter and smiles and pure enjoyment the children displayed during the games and general fun they were having. A merry time was had by all, not least by Elsa and Clare.

These parties were one of Clare's annual highlights. The children took home the carefully chosen and wrapped gifts to be opened on Christmas Day, so there was the lingering pleasure of knowing that their enjoyment would continue on Christmas Day itself.

Christmas was approaching in the MacMillan household with all the memories and expectations it brought in its wake. This was also the time of year which inevitably brought a rather formidable person into the home.

Craig's mother, Grannie Mac, was not the most popular person on earth. She and Craig could hardly be said to be close, but there was a mutual respect between them. Clare treated her mother-in-law with as much warmth as their relationship allowed, and Craig appreciated his wife's kindness to his mother.

As their boys were growing up, their grandmother cast a somewhat critical eye over their development. Taking their cue from their father, they respected her rather than loved her. Clare had decided not to try to manufacture affection towards her but made sure that basic respect toward this dignified woman was always displayed in their family.

She came to some of the boys' concerts and prize-givings but disapproved of Jerome's karate, which didn't endear her to him. She was rather conservative in her beliefs, which Clare understood and attributed to her age and personality type.

One Christmas many years ago stood out in Clare's memory.

She had invited Grannie Mac to have lunch with them, so she fetched her straight after church. She had a basketful of gifts in her hand. While Clare made tea, Grannie Mac distributed theirs to the boys. They were ten and seven at the time. Each one received his first formal shirt from his grandmother's hand. The shirts were pure white, and were accompanied by a black bowtie. Jerome was dumbstruck, Matthew was charmed. By the time Clare got to the lounge with the tea, the unwrapping had already occurred.

'Mum, look what Grannie Mac gave us,' Matthew said, excitedly.

Jerome was thoughtful and silent.

'Gosh, Mum, thank you. Do you have a specific occasion in mind?'

'My funeral, Clare, when it takes place. It could be anytime now.'

'Oh, Mum, we all hope it won't be so soon. You might not be the one to go first, you know. The world is sometimes a dangerous place for all of us.'

'I don't want this shirt, Grannie Mac. I don't like it and now it will always remind me of death. There, you can take it back to the shop,' and Jerome walked over to her and put it in her lap, and left the lounge.

'Jerome!' Clare called after him, mortified that her son could be so ungracious.

'I'll come back later, Mum. Sorry.' His apology was to her for walking out, not to his grandmother for returning her gift.

At the time, he was already doing karate, and he felt Grannie Mac's disapproval keenly. Her gift appeared to him to dictate a lifestyle. He rejected her choice as he believed she rejected his.

It was rarely that Clare felt at a loss. This was certainly such an occasion.

'Mother, we have some little gifts for you. The boys have each made you a card. I'll call Craig to join us.'

Craig was in his study—not unusually—even on Christmas morning. Clare went and briefly explained what had happened.

'She must be very hurt, darling,' she said. 'Be gentle with her, and especially attentive. Kindness from you would be the best way to make up for Jerome's outburst.'

Craig followed his wife into the lounge.

'Happy Christmas, Mother,' he said, kissing her on the cheek. His mother looked more austere than usual.

'Happy Christmas, Craig,' she responded. 'It's good to see you looking well.'

Craig's mother was always concerned when he looked pale, drawn, or stressed. That day he looked rested and relaxed.

She liked her gifts, particularly the complete volume of Jane Austen's novels which Clare had bought for her when she and Craig were in Bath. She had saved it until Christmas. It was beautifully illustrated and reminded her mother-in-law of what she and Clare had in common besides their love for Craig, of course—a mutual delight in their favourite author.

Clare excused herself from the company and went off to find Jerome, leaving Craig and his mother with their favourite, Matthew. She found Jerome lying on his bed paging through his latest book on karate, swinging his legs nonchalantly in the air as he did so.

'Hello, Mum,' he said, as she moved his desk chair closer to his bed and sat down.

'Hi, Jerome. What do you think of what happened just now with Grannie Mac, darling?'

Clare struggled to stop herself from rambling on with her own interpretation of how rude he'd been.

'I don't like it when she tries to force me to be different from what I am. I do karate. She hates that. She wants me to dress up like a nincompoop for her funeral when she's not even dead yet. I hate that.'

'Oh, I see. I can understand something of how you must have felt about her gift, but can you understand that she must be feeling very hurt at how you behaved?'

'I can stay in my room until she goes,' Jerome offered.

'No, Jerome, we are about to have Christmas lunch, probably the most special meal of the year. I'd like you to go and say sorry to Grannie Mac. Tell her that you didn't mean to be unkind.'

'Well, maybe I did. She's nasty too, even when she thinks she's being nice.'

'Jerome, please come with me. Let's tell her you didn't mean to upset her, and do you think you could ask her if you could have the shirt after all, and wear it to weddings if you're invited?'

'I don't know, Mum. I don't like shirts like that, and the bowtie is the stupidest thing I've ever seen.'

'Fine, darling, you don't ever have to wear it, but what if you just said, "Thank you for the present, Grannie Mac," and then kept it in your room till you decided you'd like to try it out, or pass it on to Elsa for someone she knows, or even kept it for a few years for Matthew to grow into?'

'Oh, and Matthew also makes me sick. He's always so goody-goody, and I know he's Grannie Mac's favourite. No, Mum, I don't want the shirt or the stupid bowtie. But I'll say sorry for upsetting her—if you think I did. She never shows how she feels so how am I supposed to know?'

'Can you do it for me, Jerome? Do you think you can? So that we can all sit down and have a happy lunch together after all?'

'Okay, Mum, I'll do it for you.'

And Clare hugged her prickly boy.

Peace was restored and lunch was a pleasant though somewhat tense affair. Matthew as always was the sweet fragrance that imbued the communal air. Craig as usual interacted minimally with his elder son, and Clare tried to make sure her mother-in-law enjoyed the occasion as much as possible under the circumstances.

Jerome and Grannie Mac's relationship never quite recovered after that. That, however, was a long time ago.

This year, 2008, Clare knew Christmas would of necessity be muted. Nicole was going through such an ordeal, as were her family and Matthew, that to be in pure celebratory mode would not be possible. Matthew wanted to spend the whole of Christmas Day with the Hayden family, so Clare decided they would have their family celebration on Christmas Eve. Nicole could join them if she felt up to it. Grannie Mac could then come for Christmas lunch with Craig and Clare the following morning after church. Clare would spare Nicole Craig's mother's occasionally abrasive manner—just in case Nicole did come.

On Christmas Eve Clare roasted a duck. It was smaller and more flavourful than a turkey. Matthew called from Nicole's house. 'Nicole's going to come with me, Mum, but we won't stay long.'

'That's fine, darling. Would it be alright if I served dinner at about seven? You could leave as soon as you needed to.'

'Seven's great, Mum. We'll come just a little while before that. Thanks for keeping things low-key. That's all Nicole can take.'

'I understand, Matthew. She'll be safe here.'

Jerome arrived, looking anxious. He was hurting for his brother. He also wasn't sure how to act around someone as seriously ill as Nicole though he realized as a medical student he'd better learn quickly.

'What shall we talk about, Mum, that doesn't relate to her illness? I don't know what to say.'

'You'll know when the time comes, Jerome, believe me you will.'

Just then Nicole stepped into the kitchen, with Matthew right behind her, his hand in the small of her back.

'Hi, Mum, hi Jerome, where's Dad?'

'He'll be here in a moment, darling. He's just busy on an important overseas call.'

'Work again, on Christmas Eve,' said Jerome, looking almost disgusted, and definitely disappointed. 'Why is his work so much more important to him than his family?'

'He works for us, Jerome, he works for us,' Clare replied, wearily. Would it never cease, this endless tussle between them?

Nicole was already seated, Matthew was attending to her tenderly, frowning at his brother for introducing a discordant note into what was to be as joyful an occasion as possible under the circumstances.

'What can I get you to drink, my love?'

'I'm only allowed water, Matthew, thank you.'

Matthew went pale, the reality of this new and strange situation hitting him between the eyes yet again. Nicole normally so enjoyed her grapetizer, her kola tonic and lemonade, her half-glass of champagne, particularly at festive occasions. But now that she'd started her course of chemotherapy, she'd been told to drink large quantities of water—and even that didn't taste good to her at present. She'd resolved to be as cooperative a patient as it was possible to be, enduring the course of chemotherapy with as much grace as she could muster.

Everyone became quiet and as if on purpose to break the silence, Craig entered the room.

'Hello Nicole, hello Matthew, hi Jerome.' He made no physical contact with any of them, but there was warmth and compassion in his tone. Clare got a light kiss, as if he'd been out rather than down the passage in his study.

'Oh, I see you already have a drink,' he said gently to Nicole. 'We guys can see to ourselves. What can I get for you, sweetheart?'

'I'll have half water, half apple juice, thank you, darling.' Clare wanted to express solidarity with Nicole without appearing too obvious.

Supper was pleasant. For Nicole's sake, Jerome didn't take on his father. He also realized that it caused his mother pain when there was friction between them. It was as though a recently healed wound was being reopened. He should desist from doing this to her. But sometimes it was as though he could not resist, as though he was driven to confront the man who had caused him such frustration and grief growing up by his lack of affirmation and intimacy. But he was beginning to realize it was mutual. He had wounded his father too, no doubt, by not conforming to society as his father expected of him.

Nicole was weak but tried to engage in conversation. She was interested in Jerome's karate classes, and in Craig's clients. For a young woman in such a distressing situation she was remarkably outgoing. But when the others talked, she became quiet, reticent, as though withdrawing into her shell of inner anguish. With the quick eye of love Matthew waited upon her every whim, including when the right time came to leave. She could not manage dessert, even though Clare had kept it to a light fruit salad and ice-cream, but wanted to sit with them as they ate. Matthew chose to skip coffee and take his beloved straight home to bed. He would wait in the Haydens' lounge while she changed and kiss her goodnight before she slept. He cherished her, Clare recognized that, and Nicole loved and appreciated him. Despite her obvious pallor, there was a quiet radiance which enfolded the two of them.

Clare found herself kissing Nicole lightly on the forehead and saying, 'We are all upholding you in prayer, Nicole. You are going to come through this ordeal wiser and stronger, you'll see . . .'

Nicole looked into Clare's eyes and smiled, bravely. They squeezed each other's hands and parted swiftly, both of them fighting back the tears.

Christmas Day itself involved a holding pattern. There was always a delicate balance which needed to be preserved when Craig and Jerome were together, and Grannie Mac was another potentially abrasive influence. Clare and Matthew were normally the glue that prevented too many sparks flying off the surfaces. With Matthew at Nicole's this year, it was all up to Clare. And it helped that she knew Jerome and Craig had both matured in their attitude to each other.

Clare and Craig went to the nearby Catholic church at ten, after which Clare dropped off at home, while Craig went to pick up his mother. The occasional frostiness between his mother and himself had mellowed into an habitual warmth.

Craig's mother was ready and waiting in the foyer.

'Hello, Mother,' Craig's lips brushed her cheek.

'Hello, Craig darling,' she said with tenderness. It was welcome to his ears, and he had to guard against responding with any kind of suspicion but rather accept her affection in good faith.

Clare was waiting for them with lunch, which included Grannie Mac's favourite baby potatoes done in olive oil, coarse salt and garnished with chives. They had a fruit punch to go with it. Big blocks of ice were at hand.

Jerome had just arrived and enjoyed a few minutes of peace and closeness with his mother.

'Mum, what are your plans for this coming year?'

'They're still evolving, Jerome. What are yours?'

'I'm planning to live a more balanced life, Mum. I think I've been too focused on my studies and karate, even though of course they are important. But I want to be more open to the personal side of life, I think . . .'

'That sounds like a healthy realization to come to, Jerome, and if this has dawned on you without exterior prompting, it must be your own deeper wisdom helping you to find greater balance. It's all about that precarious balance, darling, for all of us.'

'Yes, Mum, I guess it is.'

They were joined by Craig and his mother. Grannie Mac and Jerome had fewer sparks flying between them, it was true, but Clare never felt completely safe when they were together. Grannie Mac was certainly more likely to fly off the handle with Jerome than Craig was so Clare tried to make sure all was harmony and light. It helped that Jerome and his grandmother had both become more mellow with the years.

They had a pleasant meal, and Jerome offered to drop his grandmother home.

'Thanks, Jerome, that'll be nice. Goodbye, Mother,' and Clare kissed her mother-in-law goodbye.

Jerome and Grannie Mac spoke about his studies and, when he dropped her off, he saw her to her flat and gave her a gentle hug.

'Look after yourself, Grannie Mac,' he said, 'and don't get up to mischief.'

'I won't do anything you wouldn't do, Jerome, I promise!' Her blue eyes might be faded but they were certainly twinkling.

'See you soon, Grannie Mac. Remember you can call on me if you need a lift somewhere, especially over the weekend. I'm a bachelor and available.'

'Thanks, Jerome, I'll remember that.'

Jerome went back to his apartment feeling better about his life. He felt as though the generations before him had given him their vote of confidence.

Matthew's Christmas was playing out altogether differently. There was an atmosphere of deep sadness pervading the household. Nicole's eyes were red from crying as she was discouraged by her illness and drained by the debilitating side effects of her treatment. Her parents spoke in grave, hushed tones. Matthew wanted to bring a tone of lightness into the situation but didn't want to risk antagonising anyone. Inwardly he whispered a quick prayer for guidance.

During lunch Matthew had an inspiration. Asking Nicole's parents what music they had at their wedding served to focus the party's minds on something other than Nicole's illness.

Turning to Nicole's younger sister, Matthew said, 'Lucy, do you have your guitar handy? I'd love to play your parents' favourite piece from their wedding day. May I?'

'Of course you may, Mattthew,' Nicole's mother said, delighted that he'd come up with a plan to distract them from the overwhelming sorrow and grieving anxiety of the present.

'I'll even ask you to dance, my dear,' Nicole's father graciously suggested.

Nicole's parents waltzed charmingly to Strauss's Blue Danube, and Matthew quietly whispered a thank you to his God. His sweetheart was glowing with love for her parents and delight at Matthew's ingenuity. In a world like this, there had to be hope for her too. There simply had to be hope.

She cleared the table to prepare for dessert and kissed Matthew gently as she passed him. 'Thank you, Matthew, you've made my parents' day.'

January

Clare was sitting at the kitchen table, writing in her journal. *Of course, I could make many New Year's resolutions but, Lord, there is only one thing I truly desire, and that is to draw closer to you. So often I get distracted by the cares and preoccupations of being a mother, a wife, a sculptor, a teacher, and I know these roles are all blessings from you, but let them not pull me away from simply basking in the bliss of your love.*

New Year's Day normally brought the family together under the oaks at sunset, over punch and gammon, with plenty of salads, and strawberries and cream. January the first, 2009, was different though. Matthew was very subdued, and wanted to leave the gathering as soon as possible to go and be with Nicole, who was recovering from her chemotherapy treatment the day before. Jerome too was more sombre than usual, partly in solidarity with his brother, and partly out of envy of his brother. He inwardly longed to have someone to love with the same intensity as Matthew.

Clare only half-understood the plight of her two sons but she empathized completely with each of them. She identified with Matthew because he was so transparent and vulnerable; with Jerome because he was so complex and deep. What besides prayer could she do to help them? How could she show them she cared?

She felt a gentle reassurance that she need not strive, that they already knew beyond the shadow of a doubt that she loved them absolutely and cared for them as deeply as it was possible for a mother to do. They were her dearly beloved, right in there with her husband, and never for a moment did they desert that place, even when they were at their most difficult.

The rhythm of the MacMillan household naturally revolved partly around Craig. Even up to the present time he was highly regarded in business circles. Up and coming young businessmen sought his advice as they strove to make their mark.

His morning tea arrived in his study, occasionally delivered by Elsa, who had been working for him and Clare for most of their married life. He waited for it to stew, preferring it full-bodied, golden, rich.

His favourite disciple was Martin, a young lawyer, suave, confident, bright. He and Jerome had been good friends at school, so there was naturally a fatherly element to Craig's dealings with Martin.

Martin called him soon after New Year, saying 'Uncle Craig, can I pop round to come and discuss something with you?' Craig was pleased rather than surprised. Their talks had become customary, and he had grown to look forward to them.

'Come round, son. Later today. Tell me when it suits you.'

By the time Martin reached him, Craig had done a full day's work—attending to investments, consulting with clients, and catching up on outstanding correspondence. He was happy to see Martin's bright, young face though a cloud of concern obscured its usual expression of openness and joy.

'What's up, son?'

'It's a divorce case, Uncle Craig. The woman is beautiful. I think I'm falling in love with her. What do I do?' Martin was not one to beat about the bush.

Craig's first instinct was to laugh but his sensitivity to the pain of conflict patently evident in the young man's face made him curb it.

'Hold your horses, son, but don't deny your feelings.'

'What are you saying, Uncle Craig? Are you telling me that it is okay for a lawyer to fall in love with one of his clients?'

'Martin, I said two things. I said, hold your horses. Don't let your feelings run away with you. Secondly, I told you to be truthful about your feelings—at this point, firstly, to yourself, secondly, to me, as you have been. We may need to get Clare involved here—would that be acceptable to you?'

'I'd really appreciate her help, Uncle Craig. She'll come with a woman's perspective, and that's almost always a help.'

All Jerome and Matthew's friends called Clare by her first name while Craig was either Uncle (most intimately), or Mr

MacMillan, or simply 'sir'. Both Clare and Craig accepted this state of affairs as entirely natural.

Craig left Martin in his study while he went to check with Clare if Martin could stay to supper. Clare was more than happy to host one of Jerome's former school friends. She had always liked him for his warmth and enthusiasm.

At supper they discussed the situation. 'Do you have a girlfriend, Martin? Are you engaged to be married?' She knew they would have heard about it if Martin had got married.

'Not as such, Clare. I've had one or two relatively casual relationships but nothing serious. Suddenly I find myself bowled over by this woman I've only met a couple of times, and those times in my office in the presence of her husband! What do I do? I'm way out of my comfort zone here.'

'You take it steady, son. That's what you do. As far as the young woman is concerned, maybe Clare can be of assistance.' It always jarred with Clare when Craig so readily called Jerome's friends 'son' when he apparently found it so difficult to call Jerome himself by his proper title.

'Does she have children, Martin?' Clare asked.

'No, at least one thing is clear, Uncle Craig and Clare, and simpler than it would otherwise have been, she has no children. They've only been married for two years, and it sounds as though it was a rocky relationship right from the start. In discussions in my office it emerged that she never felt "safe enough to have children" with him.'

'So far so good,' said Craig.

'Martin, how seriously do you think you feel about this woman? Do you even know her?'

'Not at all, Clare, I barely know her at all. All I know is how she came across, with her husband, and in conflict with him, in my office. I have no one-on-one relationship with her at all. But I have never felt about any woman the way I feel about her. When I'm in her presence, I feel I can hardly breathe.'

Clare was suddenly inspired. 'Darling, what do you think? How about it if Martin passed this case on to one of his colleagues? In the course of time, as the divorce reaches its conclusion, Martin can then approach the young woman to let him get to know her?'

'Martin, you'll notice neither Clare nor I want to know the young woman's name at this point. It might work out between you and her, and it might not. We'll allow you to introduce whichever young woman you choose in your own time and way. Right now we just want to help you out of a sticky situation. I think Clare's idea is an excellent one. What do you think, son?'

'I'll definitely think about it, Clare and Uncle Craig. The downside is that way I might never set eyes on her again. But the definite upside is that it gets to be much cleaner, and if something does develop it is not out of the mire of her broken relationship with her husband. So yes, it probably is the solution. I need to think seriously which colleague to ask, one who would be good but not want to know too much about why I don't want to take the case myself. It's a good idea, Clare, thank you.'

And by this stage coffee was being served, and only a few pleasantries remained about how Jerome and Matthew were doing, and Martin's parents.

'And thank you for confiding in us, Martin. Clare and I both appreciate your trust. Let us know how things progress—only if you like, of course. But we will be interested . . .'

'And supportive,' Clare added.

Martin took his leave, feeling far lighter and less entangled than when he'd arrived, and thanking his lucky stars he had friends with parents like them.

Early the next morning Clare sat down at the kitchen table to reflect. Clare's centre of gravity was God. It was in those times that she was tempted to forget this that her world sometimes started to tremble.

Nicole's health scare presented such an occasion. She knew that for both Nicole and Matthew's sakes she needed to stay focused. But like them, she too found it very difficult territory to negotiate. She knew the secret for her was not to get drawn into the situation too much. She needed to keep some distance, some perspective, to be able to pray with a clear head and heart. They depended on her to do this. Asking questions as to why would only obfuscate the situation. She nevertheless found it well-nigh impossible to resist. So between times of faithful praying, she asked those questions and then prayed for forgiveness for doing so! Father Sean always said that it was merciful the Lord had a better sense of humour than we did. But in this situation where the health and future of a fragile young person as precious and near and dear to her as Nicole were at stake, none of the usual rules seemed to apply. And one thing she had learnt was that before God one could be most fully oneself. He was closer to us than we were to ourselves, and he knew us fully. We could keep no secrets from him.

So by the time Craig surfaced—almost always later than herself—she had made peace with the situation and her feelings about it, and had hope for the future for Nicole and for Matthew.

It was not so simple for Matthew though. At the same time that his parents were saying their good mornings to each other, he was gazing into the goldfish pond. Like his mother, he sometimes came here to commune with God or to reflect on perplexing issues. What was happening in his life? Tears were streaming down his face, and he noticed he was wringing his hands in anguish. He didn't care, as he knew this was a safe

32

and private place. Only his mother may find him here, and there was no self-consciousness between them.

He prayed for Nicole and for her complete recovery. He prayed for himself too, that he would release her fully into the hands of God, in whatever form that might take. He realized afresh that this was the woman he wanted to marry and have children with. He promised to dedicate their children to God if he would spare her, if he would have mercy on them and grant them a future together.

He allowed his heart to subside before he went to the kitchen to have a final cup of tea with his mother before setting out for his first appointment and then another visit to Nicole. His father would already be seated at his desk. He wasted no time in the morning getting started.

'Hello, Matthew darling,' Clare said as Matthew walked into the kitchen. She reached out her arms to him and embraced her tall son, no longer a little boy but oh, so vulnerable. She longed to still his aching heart. Words seemed better left unspoken but her empathy was palpable and Matthew derived so much strength from her, and Nicole in turn from him.

His older brother was facing challenges of an altogether different nature. A couple of weeks into the new year, Luca came up to Jerome after the karate class.

'Sensei, would you come to my house for supper next week? My mother wants to thank you for your kindness to me.'

'I'll tell you at our next class, Luca. Please thank your mother for the invitation.'

As grown up as he was, this was the kind of decision Jerome discussed with his mother.

'Go, Jerome, for Luca's sake.'

'But Mum, you know how clingy divorced women can be. And I'd hate to hurt Luca and make his personal situation worse. Who knows what might be going through his mind?'

'Go, Jerome, and be courteous but on your guard.'

'Mum, I'll follow your advice this time, but I sure hope it's sound.'

'Trust me in this, Jerome. Your focus and the mother's focus will be on her son.'

'This is where I wish I had a girlfriend, Mum. Then I could have taken her with me, wouldn't that have made things clear?'

'Yes, Jerome, you know that even as a child you were in my prayers as far as a partner for you was concerned. And she will emerge, darling, and you will know when she does.'

'I hope that time is not too far away . . .'

'When you are ready, she will appear. Rest in that assurance.'

Daniela opened the door for Jerome and Luca. Slender, with long black hair and an olive complexion, she showed Jerome to a chair in the lounge and offered him a drink.

'Firstly, Mr Jerome, may I thank you for being so kind to Luca? He so looks forward to his karate classes and his chats with you.'

'Mrs Romano, please call me Jerome.'

'And you may call me Daniela then.'

And so the preliminaries were settled. Luca hovered between them and all that lay ahead of them was the rest of the evening.

This getting to know each other was nothing less than daunting. How would they fill up the time? Luca clearly wanted them to get on, and whatever else he might be hoping for one could only imagine.

'What work do you do, Daniela?' Jerome asked, trying to play it safe.

'I work in a children's library,' she responded, 'and greatly enjoy it. I have written several children's books myself, so am a keen student of children's reading styles, their likes and dislikes.'

'Have you written them in Italian?' Jerome asked.

'Yes, but all of them except the most recent one have been translated into English. I am considering doing the translation myself this time because I have learnt a lot of English in the last few years but don't want to spoil the story with a poor translation. I think Luca will be able to help me.'

'I said I would, Mama, and I will if you give it to me.'

'It's a sad story, Luca, and I'm not sure if I'm ready to let you read it.'

'Mama, I'm thirteen. You let seven-year-olds read your books.'

'I know, Luca, but you're my son. You see, Jerome, we've been through a difficult time, Luca and I. I think he's told you, so I don't like reminding him of it.'

'Luca has spoken to me, Daniela, but only in the most general of terms.'

'And that's good, Luca. I'm glad you haven't burdened your sensei with our problems.'

'Sensei, what do I call you when we're at our home? What do you want me to call you?'

'Just call me Jerome, Luca. I know in class you won't forget to call me "Sensei", will you?'

'No, Jerome, I won't. And thank you. It is great that I can call you by your real name.'

When it was time for dinner, Daniela brought a most delicious dish of lasagne to the table, served with a Greek salad Luca had helped to make earlier. Tiramisu was served for dessert, followed by espresso. Luca helped Daniela serve and clear. Jerome was instructed to stay seated and be waited on.

When it was time to leave, Jerome extended his hand to Daniela and said, 'Next time I'd like to take you and Luca out for dinner.'

'Thank you, Jerome, we'd love that.'

'I shall arrange a suitable time through Luca,' Jerome said.

'Or take my number, Jerome, please do.'

'Okay, that makes sense. Thanks. Then goodnight.'
'Goodbye, Jerome. Thanks for coming.'

The next day Daniela sat on her balcony overlooking the park in Kenilworth where they lived. There was a see-saw, some swings, a jungle gym and a roundabout, frequented by the children of the neighbourhood. Some of these used the library where she worked. Some were even potential readers of her books.

But right now she was not thinking of them. No, her thoughts were of Jerome and the evening they had spent together. And of Luca. Luca was never far from her thoughts, and his well-being was of paramount importance to her. The sense of comfort and security he displayed around Jerome buoyed her up. It formed a counterbalance to the dread which hit her in the pit of her stomach whenever Antonio, her ex-husband, crossed her mind. He was supposed to be living and working in Naples but she never knew when he'd land in Cape Town and come and harass her and Luca.

So what was Jerome all about? she wondered. She realized how vulnerable she was, how easily she fell in love—always had done. If only she could find *one* man she could exclusively devote herself to, and who would love her, and Luca, and whom she could trust, and be safe with. Could this happen? She knew she needed a man in her life who was stable, not someone like

Antonio who was even worse than she was. She prayed that she would not let her imagination run wild, but that she would be steady, if not for her own sake, then for Luca's.

Like Clare, Daniela felt better after praying but, unlike Clare, she lived her life on a rollercoaster of emotion, her moods frequently fluctuating between ecstasy and despair.

She finished her coffee and went back to her writing at the computer. Luca would soon be home from his afternoon maths class. She was thankful that he was getting on top of his maths, and that he had some good friends. She longed to make their home a safe haven for him.

Luca found his mother calm and smiling when he got home. *Oh, thank goodness, she's not in one of her moods.* He returned home daily with anxiety about the state of mind in which he would find his mother.

'Hello, Luca, how was maths?' Daniela started arranging his lunch.

'It's getting easier, it's definitely getting easier, Mama.' She could hear the relief in his voice.

They spent a productive afternoon and evening together, working on their respective projects, exchanging ideas here and there, with one of Luca's friends joining them for supper to finish off an assignment on ecology.

Daniela went to sleep contented, thankful for Luca and his development, and with a tremor of suspense in relation to Jerome.

The next day she felt refreshed and invigorated and enjoyed her work in the library.

Jerome and Clare arranged to meet for coffee. There was a cafeteria at the medical campus of UCT where they occasionally met between lectures and practicals.

'How did it go?' Clare asked, without further ado.

'It was a wonderful evening, Mum, once the initial awkwardness had been gotten over. She's a children's author, and librarian, and she's very attractive. I like the way she and Luca relate. I found myself inviting the two of them out for dinner. I wish you could come as well, then you could tell me what you think.'

Clare laughed. 'There'll be time enough for that, darling, if anything develops, and you don't yet know that it will, do you now?'

'No, Mum, I don't, but I'm half-afraid it will. And I can ill afford any distraction from my studies.'

'You're jumping the gun, Jerome. Take it one step at a time. She is the mother of one of your students, she invited you to dinner, and now you are reciprocating. For the moment let that be all there is to it. There's plenty of time ahead for things to develop if they need to.'

'Thanks, Mum. You always calm me down. I really don't want to mess up my studies.'

'You won't, Jerome, I trust you not to.'

As she had promised Matthew, Clare contacted Nicole's mother Pam and they occasionally met for tea. The state of Nicole's health and progress was uppermost in both their minds.

'She's not responding too well to the chemotherapy, Clare. It is not that the chemo itself might not be effective, but she finds the accompanying nausea and fatigue extremely debilitating, and as a result she struggles to have a positive attitude to it.'

'We'll continue our prayers—both for the effectiveness of the treatment and also for her to feel differently about it. It is such a challenge when she is used to feeling energetic and healthy.'

They discussed everything except their children's romance. This was clearly off limits. Pam and her family (like Grannie Mac) were ardent Presbyterians.

'Pam, I think I might have mentioned the interdenominational prayer and Bible study group I belong to. We meet at the houses of various members. Next week it's at our house. Would you like to come?'

'Thank you, Clare, I think I would. Nicole and the rest of us could do with all the prayer support possible at this time, and the Bible study group I used to be part of has recently dissolved. Various members moved from the area, or emigrated. So maybe this could be my new group. When is it?'

'It's on Thursdays, at three.'

'I'll be there. Thank you.'

'Why don't you come a few minutes early, Pam? I think that'll make introductions easier and more gradual for you.'

'Thanks, Clare. I'll do so.'

'Oh, and we have tea afterwards. So we're normally done by about four-thirty.'

Thursday came soon enough and Pam arrived about fifteen minutes early. She and Clare sat down quietly to talk for a few minutes before the others arrived.

Introductions were duly done, and the women settled down to prayer. Nothing specific was mentioned about Nicole's needs, but the new member of the group was welcomed, in prayer as well, and it was hoped that the group would be a blessing to her and her family. Pam felt warmed and welcome.

'Stay for another cup of tea afterwards, just today, please, Pam,' Clare requested.

Pam went to freshen up and came through to the kitchen where Clare was reviving the pot of tea.

'Pam, I'd like you and me to join hands and pray for Nicole. We both do so daily, probably hourly in your case, and I do believe combined prayer is even more effective.'

They joined hands and committed the situation to the God they both served, and both had deeper peace thereafter. They hugged goodbye, and Pam was getting into her car just as Craig drove into the gate.

'Shall I stay to greet Craig?' Pam asked.

'Entirely up to you.'

'I think I won't, Clare, if he won't mind.'

But Craig was already at her car window. He reached in to press her hand. 'We're with you in this, Pam,' he reassured her. 'We pray for Nicole and all of you daily.'

Clare was grateful to hear these reassuring words from her husband. It was not often that he spoke about his Christian faith in explicit terms.

Over supper, Craig asked Clare how her meeting had been.

'Good, thanks. Pam fitted in well, I think. How was your afternoon?'

'Fine, it was one of my clients' business conferences, and he wanted me to do a short presentation, which I did. It was well received.'

'Oh, I'm so glad to hear that. Darling, I think it might be a good idea to ask Matthew whether he'd like to bring Nicole to supper again one evening. They need our support at this impossibly difficult time.'

'I agree, sweetheart. I have no further engagements this week, and next week only my Tuesday evening commitment.'

'Good. Then I'll call Matthew straight after dinner and he can see when Nicole's available.'

Clare and Matthew settled on the following Wednesday, halfway between two chemotherapy sessions for Nicole. She had one every two weeks.

'Please continue praying, Mum,' Matthew said over the phone. 'The whole situation is terrible for her. Her illness scares her and she sees the treatment as her enemy rather than her friend.'

'We all are praying, darling. And Pam was here today for prayer and Bible study. She's participating in my group so we can join forces.'

'Oh, that's good to know, Mum.'

When Wednesday came, Nicole arrived with Matthew, looking very frail. Matthew was very gentle with her, as were Craig and Clare.

She spoke very little, but smiled occasionally if something humorous was said. Craig always appreciated it when someone enjoyed his wry humour.

After supper the four of them joined hands and prayed.

Individually they went to sleep that night more at peace than before.

February

It's hot, Lord, and we all get irritable. Help us to be gentle with each other. Thank you that you are actively involved in the healing process Nicole is undergoing. Your grace and the wonder of your love are not hampered by illness or disease. Instead you turn these curses around to become vehicles by which you demonstrate your glory and your grace. Thank you, dearest Lord.

Clare knew it was time to go for confession when she started to feel stale and unenthusiastic, when a pall of habit and sameness settled over her. It was then that she knew she was in danger of losing her 'first love', that intimate, passionate devotion to Christ referred to by St John in Revelation.

Father Sean would help her over this hurdle and into the next phase, she felt confident. But she knew she only had to whisper her sorrow inwardly and her soul would be renewed. Her sorrow was already a sign of grace from God. Father Bernard had told her this long ago, before his passing, and she returned to this thought periodically. It was like unwrapping a pearl, which was in the shape of a tear. She had been taught that God stored our tears in a bottle, and this had consoled her on many occasions, especially in the years when she grieved over the distance between Craig and Jerome.

In espousing the principles of karate, Jerome had turned his attention away from Catholicism but had not turned his back on Christianity. He combined principles of pacifism from both philosophies and considered himself a karate instructor who was also a Christian. Clare had no problem with this. Craig was less flexible.

'Why does he embrace a philosophy from the East?' he would mutter in a disgruntled fashion.

'Why shouldn't he? God rules over East and West.'

'He rules over those of us who submit to his Lordship, sweetheart, and you know that.'

Clare hated it when Craig spoke to her as if she were a child. But she clung with rugged determination to Jerome's right to live according to his own beliefs. She was only too grateful that he hadn't cast Christianity aside, and she knew he had made a conscious decision not to. But that he had chosen to construct his own unique set of convictions was something she was in fact very proud of, and she would support his freedom to do so every time.

A couple of weeks after his first supper with Daniela and Luca, on a Friday night, Jerome picked them up and took them to a quiet steakhouse which he believed they would both enjoy. Once they'd ordered he turned to Daniela.

'Have you made any progress on getting your latest book translated?' he asked.

'Yes, Luca and I have done some talking. He's willing to help me.'

'But first Mum has to let me read the book, Jerome, and she's not yet ready to let me do that. She thinks it will upset me.'

'Oh, I see . . .'

'In time it will happen, Jerome. I am patient. I am so grateful Luca is willing to assist. We shall have fun together eventually.'

'Yes, Mama, anytime you are ready so am I.'

Jerome laughed. 'You have a keen translator on your side, Daniela! Don't keep him waiting too long. He might sell his services elsewhere.'

'No, I won't do that, Jerome, I promise. I'll wait for Mama. But I wish she would realize I'm not a little boy anymore. I'm a teenager and can handle whatever she's written. I'm sure I've already experienced worse.' And his face clouded over. Jerome realized they were on dangerous ground, and changed the subject to the menu.

'Do you know what you're going to eat yet, Luca? Daniela? Can I tell you about some of my favourites?'

The atmosphere eased, Luca realized how hungry he was, and Jerome and Daniela exchanged adult glances, in which mutual concern for the state of mind of their young charge was expressed.

The joys of pizza to a teenager prevailed, and while Jerome and Daniela got to know each other, Luca was fairly focused on getting through his large, ambitious meal. He triumphed.

Jerome and Daniela were developing an affinity for each other, and both knew intuitively that this would be the first date of many.

Alone at the goldfish pond, Clare pondered some of the differences between her two sons. She knew the books on parenting did not recommend this but she had always found it the most natural thing in the world to do, and it helped her understand each of them better, she believed. Between Matthew and Clare there was an intuitive understanding. They spoke often, with Matthew getting more animated as he got older, more articulate, and more separate from Clare. Jerome, on the other hand, got quieter, more introverted.

Jerome was taking longer to find his feet. Clare was well aware of this, and believed that the best way to handle it was to take a backseat, to be available but not intrusive. Nevertheless, Jerome was her firstborn, and as such had turned Clare into a mother. Their bond was naturally intense.

Craig, on the other hand, had experienced their first baby as something of an intruder. He had previously revelled in his wife's total availability, her warm attention, her interest, her constant presence whenever he required it. Suddenly there was a vociferous bundle of needs demanding her urgent presence, necessitating that she drop whatever she was busy with, even if it was attending to her husband. He found it difficult not to resent this.

This tension set the tone for Craig's relationship with his elder son. Even when Jerome grew up to be an independent young man, Craig always felt they were vying for Clare's attention. Their relationship was distant and cool rather than warm and close. It stopped short of being hostile but it lacked intimacy.

Entirely different was Craig's relationship with Matthew. Already a mother, Clare coped with her new baby's needs in a far more relaxed way than she had with her first.

Jerome had always felt somewhat alienated from his father. He would have believed that was how father-son relationships were supposed to be had it not been for Matthew's comfortable understanding with Craig and the close, easy relationships one or two of his friends had with their fathers. He was disappointed and he knew his mother was too. But there was very little indication that Craig himself was seeking a greater closeness with his elder son.

Clare regularly resolved to stop trying to improve their relationship. But it seemed she couldn't help herself. She so wanted them to have a deeper understanding, more intimacy. She believed that this lack was one of the major causes of Jerome's reserve. In part it was no doubt due to his personality but surely the absence of affirmation from his father contributed to him feeling less than safe in a hostile world. Also Craig was missing out on the intimacy he could be experiencing with his son.

'Sweetheart, why don't you and Jerome go out and do something together? Go to a cricket match, or go and watch a karate performance with him. I'm sure you'll both enjoy it.'

'It's not necessary, Clare,' he said coolly. 'Jerome's old enough to pursue his interests by himself, and I'm old enough to pursue mine. I'd rather go to a cricket match with you, my darling.' Now his voice was soft and gentle.

Inwardly she sighed. She knew she had better stop trying. It hurt her, caused strain between her and Craig, and when Jerome realized here or there what efforts she was making, it presumably made his sense of rejection worse. This was one situation she found it very difficult to accept. She questioned herself as to how she may have contributed.

Yet all I ever wanted was to be a harmonious family, with my sons having healthy relationships with both their parents, she said to herself. *Lord, heal whatever hurt or mistrust there may be, and help me stay out of it to whatever extent is necessary, and please enable me to do or say the right thing where it would be helpful. I don't want to interfere, Lord, but I can sense Jerome is hurting. There seems no need, Lord, for this rift to be there.*

And Clare would feel a little calmer, less burdened, more hopeful. And it would help relieve the strain among the three of them.

With Matthew all was sunshine and uncomplicated.

Matthew said, 'Mum, I don't think you should interfere,' when she confided her concerns to him. 'This is man stuff.

Let them work it out. Maybe they are comfortable with the level they are at. You could hurt yourself—as you already are by taking this upon yourself—and you could actually make it worse between them by making them self-conscious about how they relate. Leave it, little one, leave it.'

Ever since he was small, Matthew had endearing names for her. The first picture he drew at nursery school of himself and his mother showed them to be exactly the same size, like two friends of the same age. Clare loved this, Craig disapproved.

'You need to remedy this, Clare, forthwith. No child should see his mother as his equal. It leads to a breakdown of authority later, if not immediately. My mother was a child psychologist, remember? I know these things.'

Craig knew everything. Clare had long ago accepted this. There was nothing he was not an authority on. *Lord Jesus, help me to handle this and simply to appreciate having a husband who is so knowledgeable.*

She tried not to argue with Craig unless their difference of opinion was on a vital matter, and she had in any case learnt to treat herself with some degree of scepticism. Clare had recently come across a quotation in *Middlemarch* which had even altered her perception of her own prayers:

> *Does any one suppose that private prayer is necessarily candid—necessarily goes to the roots of action? Private prayer is inaudible speech, and speech is representative: who can represent himself just as he is, even in his own reflections?*

After being taken aback for a moment and pondering the truth of it, she had nevertheless decided to continue praying as before, only with the awareness that there lurked even in her own heart more guile than she had previously thought.

It was true that Craig was sometimes irritable with his wife. Her concern for their sons occasionally seemed excessive to him. He knew mothers loved their children differently from fathers, but surely Clare took it too far. Jerome after all was already twenty-seven. Other men had married and had children by that age, and had bought a house and were paying the mortgage. Perhaps Jerome would be doing the same if Clare did not fuss so much. Craig did not often express these sentiments but Clare had a fair idea of how he thought about her relationship with their sons. And she didn't like it.

'Allow me the freedom to relate to Jerome and Matthew the way I see fit, Craig. They are my sons too, and I have to be allowed to love them as a mother. It is a love I do not expect you to understand—I do not mean to be condescending, only realistic—you cannot know what it is to be a mother. I try to give you untrammelled access to them—and forgive me if ever I seem to stand between you and them—it is not my intention—but I expect no less from you. Even your criticism hurts me and throws me off my stride. It is difficult enough for me to know how best to relate to them without having to look over my shoulder and worry about your opinion too.'

'Sorry, sweetheart, I do not mean to cramp your style or make you uptight. I only want what is best for all of us, the boys included. And sometimes I think you fuss too much.'

'That is exactly the kind of opinion I find unhelpful. It is critical and hurtful. I do what mothers do, and I do it the best I know how.'

'But when do you let go, sweetheart, and allow them to lead their own lives?'

'When I'm six feet under, that's when. While they need me—or in any way want my input in their lives—I plan to be available to them. It would be better for you to accept this, or else we will simply have endless conflict and nothing will change.'

These talks were generally humourless, while each of them became more dogged in their determination that their view of the situation was the correct one. Invariably Clare ended up praising Craig for the great job he'd done as a father, and reminding him of her and their sons' appreciation of him, and asking him in turn to trust her. She would not be the proverbial castrating mother and undo the manhood of the sons he was so proud of.

'If they can handle and welcome my presence in their lives, so should you, darling. Let's agree to give this topic a rest. Trust me. Please do. And trust Jerome and Matthew—they are not going to allow themselves to be emasculated. We appreciate one another, that's all—always have done, and I pray we always will. Now let's play a game of scrabble over a mug of milo.'

'I'd prefer a glass of whisky, Clare. You forget I'm a grown man. But scrabble sounds good. Let's see if I know how to spell "maternal"!'

She punched him lightly on the arm, they organized their respective drinks, and sat down to a tension-relieving game of scrabble. Craig always preferred it when he won.

Sundays had become days of reflection, days of peace, and sometimes family days, with Grannie Mac occasionally coming to lunch or tea. Clare's parents had always tried to make Sundays special—by going to church together, cooking a roast, and mostly not working. They did things together as a family, like going to Kirstenbosch Gardens, or the beach, or simply relaxing at home, over scrabble, or a game of chess. Clare and Craig had tried to do roughly the same. Only as teenagers had the boys become slightly resistant to these traditions on principle—the principle that at this stage any family tradition got questioned and potentially rejected—but once the day was flowing, they enjoyed themselves nevertheless.

Today was another Sunday. Jerome had been asked to join in for lunch even though Grannie Mac was invited.

'Will Matthew be there?' he asked on the phone when Clare called him.

'No, Matthew will be having lunch with Nicole's family, Jerome, but it would be great for Grannie Mac to have at least one of her grandsons present. Matthew is often here without you. Can't you make it, darling?'

'Okay, Mum, I'll come for lunch but I don't have time to linger afterwards. I'm working on an assignment that needs to be in by Tuesday.'

'That's fine, Jerome. I understand. Just seeing you for even a short while will do us all good.'

'Don't speak for Dad, Mum. You think you know the man. You don't know him the way I do.'

'Darling, let's not go that route. Just show up, and let's all enjoy being together as best we can.'

On Sunday Craig picked up his mother, and Jerome arrived as promised.

Conversation flowed. Everyone was on their best behaviour.

'How are your studies going, Jerome?' Grannie Mac asked.

'Fine, thanks, Grannie Mac. A lot of work, but it's quite rewarding.'

'You'll make a great doctor, Jerome,' Craig volunteered. 'You have the right combination of seriousness and compassion.'

Clare almost fainted. *Thank you, Lord—only you could have put those words in his mouth.*

Jerome flushed with pleasure.

'Thanks, Dad,' he whispered hoarsely.

Over coffee in the lounge, Jerome found a moment to speak to his mother alone, while Craig and Grannie Mac were wandering down memory lane, remembering the days when Craig's father was still alive.

'Mum, I need your input.' Jerome spoke softly, to avoid getting his grandmother's opinion instead. 'There's a competition in my Diagnostics class. Only ten students are allowed to enter—we all work with a different patient—and I've been invited. But I'm so apprehensive—nervous that I won't win, and nervous that I might win. What do you think I should do?'

'What is there to lose, darling? Even if you don't win, all you will lose is a bit of pride. You will still be richer for the experience. Just being invited is an honour. Well done! I'd say go for it, Jerome. As I see it, you have nothing to lose. Just go for the experience.'

'Thanks, Mum, I'll think about it. You're probably right. I'm afraid to lose face before my peers.'

'And yet you've already been invited to participate and most of them have not. So you're already in the "top ten", as it were. Just enjoy the experience, and let me know how it all turns out.'

'Will do, Mum,' and Jerome said his goodbyes. Just a cordial handshake between him and his father, but Clare had trained herself not to expect great warmth and hugs between them.

She saw Jerome off to his car. They embraced, and he kissed her lightly on the lips. She watched his car out of the driveway and into the big world, where she could accompany him no longer, touched that he had confided in her. *Bless him,*

Lord, and may he know your provision and guidance, now and throughout his life.

She joined her husband and mother-in-law, secure in the love of her son.

Clare's keeping of a journal over the years helped encourage her through difficult times. It reminded her that bad news was most often not the end of a story.

Craig respected her need for reflection. By contrast, he saw himself as a man of action, someone whose thoughts translated into deeds often without passing through the somewhat cumbersome medium of words. Clare in turn respected his more action-oriented way though frequently regretted his preference to short-circuit a conversation with a unilateral decision.

Craig 'knew' he was right. He did not feel the need to discuss an issue and consider other angles. One point of view was enough, and that was his, the perfect one. Normally, of course, he was right, but there were those other, more complex times, when Clare longed for a deeper openness between them, where her perspective would be listened to, carefully considered, responded to, and not dismissed out of hand, before it had even been uttered, simply because it was different from the authoritative point of view of her husband.

When their sons were small, there had been conflicts over their different styles of negotiating life—her leisurely, reflective style versus Craig's decisive line of command. Particularly, issues surrounding the handling of Jerome, a more complicated child than Matthew, caused conflict as Craig tended to be uncompromising while Clare appreciated the many angles to a difficult question.

Once Jerome left home, conflict abated markedly. There was palpable relief all round at not having to deal with Jerome's intense moods, which raged from manic cheer to hostility and depression. Clare was close to both her sons, and so it pained her when they were unhappy. While Jerome was often hard to read, Matthew was sanguine and pleasant, with only brief and always comprehensible spells of sadness.

Now was of course such a time. The side effects of the course of chemotherapy Nicole was undergoing, the acute nausea, and feeling utterly weak and drained, were unpleasant not only for her but for all concerned. As long as the treatment was effective, and successful, Clare kept on admonishing Matthew, it would all be worth it.

Clare closed her eyes and called a halt to her anxious thoughts. She would release them, Matthew and Nicole, to find their way through this. She knew they loved the Lord, and loved each other. She could not ask for more. Or could she? Yes, healing for Nicole. And she would pray for this fervently, along with Nicole's family, and of course Matthew.

Lord, I see her whole, healthy, and at peace. Bring her through this, dear Lord, with a deeper faith in you and your love for her.

Help her not to waver, not to give in. Help her to know you have her best possible good at heart, her best possible good in mind. Help her to cling onto this and receive the healing you surely have in store for her.

There were burning questions unanswered, Clare knew that, for Nicole, for Matthew, for her whole family, Nicole's mother in particular. But they all needed to cling to the Rock, which was Christ. Could they? Would they? It was their only hope. So she would pray for them too, that they would be strong, on Nicole's behalf, at this almost unbearably difficult time.

Clare sat quietly, allowing her fears to subside, as she received comfort, and as peace suffused her being. She never ceased to admire people who could negotiate their way through life without this sense of God's presence. For her, it was what enabled her to continue from one hour to the next.

For Jerome, things had been moving along at a pace. It was late one Saturday night. Luca had already gone to bed. Daniela and Jerome were enjoying a cup of hot chocolate when he gently took her hands into his own.

'I'd like permission to court you,' he said, and looked at her intently. 'Could you accept that, Daniela? How would that feel for you? And of course for Luca?'

'For once since Luca was born, I am going to think only of myself. I would love that, Jerome, I truly would. In fact, in my mind, at some level, we've been courting already.'

Jerome kissed her, for the first time, gently, with affection and tenderness. No passionate expression for them at this time. They were very careful and, of course, despite Daniela's denial, they both thought very much of Luca, who could walk into the room at any moment. What would they tell him?

But for this one evening they both wanted to focus on themselves alone. It was new to Jerome, to be involved with a woman at a level which could only be serious. There was no other way. She was older than him, and their needs might be different. Could they find a path through the challenges they would most certainly encounter? Of Antonio neither of them even wanted to think.

'What would you expect of me, Daniela? And could you accept that I still have a long road of studying before me?' He did not want to say, 'I couldn't settle down till then,' because settling down may not be where things would lead. Would Daniela—and Luca—be able to handle disappointment if the relationship did not work out? That was his greatest fear.

Daniela simply basked in the bliss that this step of Jerome's signified for her. She already loved him, there was no doubt in her heart or mind about that. That he could allow himself to have feelings for her—and act on them—this was a dream come true. She realized the greatest challenge at this stage would be for her to keep steady and not to scare Jerome away with too much intensity. Could she hold herself to this? She hoped she would.

For Matthew and Nicole things appeared to be less rosy. Nicole unexpectedly had to spend a night in hospital. She had contracted flu and quickly become dehydrated. The doctors were taking no chances. She needed to spend the night in hospital to be stabilised. Clare waited in the hospital reception foyer for Matthew to come and tell her when Nicole was ready to be visited. This was Nicole's second stay in hospital since the onset of her illness, and Clare's hope was—if all went according to the best possible medical prognosis—it would be her last. This was Clare's first visit. Previously when Nicole had spent a couple of nights in hospital at the beginning of her treatment, she had been too unwell to receive any visitors except her parents and Matthew.

Clare watched the comings and goings of people entering and leaving the hospital. The end of the evening visiting hour was approaching. She was particularly touched by one elderly gentleman seeing off his wife, who had been to visit him. He held her hand for a long time, as she stooped to kiss his cheek. He was in a wheelchair but seemed independent enough, wheeling himself around after she left to conceal the tear that Clare had already seen. How would Craig and I handle a situation like this? she asked herself. She quickly realized that was a bridge only to be crossed should they get there. She felt the Lord's chastising whisper as quick and quiet as a lightning flash. *Sorry, Lord, help me not to speculate but to live in your moment. And right now it's all about Nicole, and about Matthew.*

No sooner had she thought this than Matthew appeared. 'She's ready for you, Mum,' he said with a bright smile. 'Don't stop your prayers please!'

'Of course I won't, darling. I pray for you all daily, and most especially at this time for Nicole. And God hears our prayers, remember, and hastens to answer them even before they have left our hearts . . .'

Nicole smiled as Clare entered. She looked frail but happy. 'Please sit here, Auntie Clare,' and she beckoned to the chair closest to her. 'Thank you for coming to see me. That is so nice of you. And thank you for your prayers. Matthew and my mum have told me how steadfast you have been. I do appreciate it, and the Lord is answering. I know he is.'

'I had no doubt he would, sweet Nicole,' and Clare laid her hand reassuringly over Nicole's. 'How are you feeling? How is it going with the treatment?'

'I often feel really grim, Auntie Clare, that is true. But both doctors who are treating me are happy with my progress, and that is all that matters.' And now tears welled up in her eyes. 'I thought I was going to die, Auntie Clare, I really did, and I wasn't ready for that. I am so young. I have my studies. Above all, I have Matthew and the hope we share for our future. So I couldn't accept that my life was over. I simply couldn't.'

'Of course you couldn't, dearest Nicole, and we're all so glad you didn't. You fought against this disease, you cooperated with the doctors and their instructions, and ultimately with the Lord himself, to overcome it. You have done well. We are all proud of you, aren't we, Matthew?'

Matthew himself was between smiles and tears. It was a deep joy to him to see the two women he most loved in conversation. His tears were a mingling of sadness and relief at what Nicole had been through and was still going through. But more than ever, despite the touch of flu and dehydration, today was a day filled with hope as interim tests contained promising news. And his mother's presence made victory seem all the more likely.

After more chatting and laughing, still not without tears, they prayed together before Clare left. She had come in her own car, and so could leave Matthew with Nicole. 'I'll leave when she needs to get her medication and have a sleep. Thanks for coming, Mum.' Matthew had permission to pay Nicole extended visits.

Driving home Clare was hugely relieved. Though frail, Nicole had an inner strength and a complete trust that her healing was in process.

At supper Clare told Craig of her visit. He was delighted, though showed it in few words, and a relieved sigh. 'She is a lovely girl. What would Matthew do without her? It would devastate him.'

'Yes, darling, they belong together, it's as simple as that. They go such a long way back, and I believe they have a long, hopefully happy road to travel together.'

'Now, sweetheart, don't you get involved with how long or how happy. Let them be the best judge of that!'

'I know, darling, I know. I'm not about to play *deus ex machina* like your mother.'

A slight frown crossed Craig's brow. As much as he hated his mother's interference, he also didn't like Clare to criticize her, even in veiled terms, but certainly not explicitly like now.

'Sorry, darling.' She was quick to touch his arm to try and coax him back to good humour.

'She called me today, Clare, and sounded lonely. Can you invite her over, sweetheart? Do you think we could do a special dinner for her birthday next week, on the 9th? Do you have anything on then? I checked, and I don't.'

'We can certainly make a plan, darling. Sorry, I didn't mean to sound disrespectful. It just slipped out.'

'Yes, Clare, resorting to Latin to criticize my mother is unlike you. And she's getting on now. We need to be more tolerant.'

Clare was not used to being reprimanded by her husband, but when he did it, he usually had justice on his side. Like now. And she had realized over the years that he did not like to be protected from his mother by Clare. He felt he could handle her himself, and preferred to do so.

Jerome and Matthew were both available. Clare decided to keep the party to the five of them. Grannie Mac really could stir the pot, and she didn't think either Daniela, by all accounts, or Nicole were robust enough at the moment to withstand the onslaught.

It was a Monday evening. Matthew arrived first, with a box of chocolates for his grandmother. 'You can enjoy these at your next bridge party, I hope, Grannie Mac.' And Jerome, looking rushed, entered with a bunch of roses. He and his grandmother had learnt to respect each other's differences but there were still times they riled each other. 'These are to make up for any bad feelings, Grannie Mac. You know I love you.' It was most unusual for Jerome to express feelings so openly. Is Daniela's Italian influence rubbing off on him? Clare wondered. It might be a very good thing and help him become more relaxed, less defensive. Clare held her breath in anticipation of what this new relationship might hold in store for her son.

Grannie Mac enjoyed being the centre of attention and having her family spoil her. This time it was Craig who wanted to take her home, to give her some personal son-to-mother reassurances.

About a week later Craig and Clare were sitting down at the dinner table. She cooked most nights but he had a few favourite dishes he enjoyed preparing a couple of times a month. Spaghetti bolognaise was one, and lamb chops with mash and vegetables another. Simple but nourishing. Tonight it was lamb with glazed carrots and green beans.

The mood, however, was sombre. Craig had just learnt that Jerome was dating an Italian divorcée, six years older than himself, with a teenage son. He was less than impressed. But then again, he was seldom impressed by Jerome.

'Have you met her?' he asked Clare.

'Not yet,' she replied, 'but I thought I might meet her for coffee one of these days. If it gets more serious we could have them over for a meal.'

'I hope it doesn't get more serious. What is Jerome thinking? He seems unable to think clearly on most things.' Craig seemed despondent.

'I think you're too hard on him, Craig. He's undertaken an ambitious course of study, has been largely supporting himself for years, and is now dating a woman of his choice. What more could we ask for?'

'That he embarked on a decent course of study from the word go instead of pursuing his weird karate, and that he dates a normal South African girl of the same age or younger.'

'I think you're being very prescriptive, darling, if you don't mind my saying so.'

Craig looked hurt, and taken aback. He was not used to being criticized by his wife. He remained silent.

In a conciliatory tone she continued: 'I think Jerome is the kind of person who needs to find his own way, without interference or too much input from his parents or even friends. He has always been very independent, and a bit of a loner. Who knows what will make him happy? How do we know what kind of a wife he needs? I think we shouldn't judge until we meet her, and even then we need to remember that it's his choice, and that whichever way things go, he'll have to live with it.'

Craig remained silent.

Clare hated it when he did this, when he withdrew into himself to punish her. But she'd come to realize that she just had to be patient and in a while things would get back to normal. So she gently changed the subject to cricket, usually a safe subject, and certainly one of Craig's passionate interests, alongside his work.

The topic of cricket helped tide them over. In her many years of being married to Craig, Clare had picked up more than the basics and was able to have an intelligent conversation about the game, although the personalities of the players interested her more than what kind of ball was bowled or hit. She deferred—as she did in many other things—to Craig's better judgment. When it came to cricket and economics, she was more than ready to do so. The one area in which she could not relinquish her own insights or instincts was in matters pertaining to their sons. She believed she was closer to them, particularly to Jerome, than Craig was, and that she had a better intuitive understanding of their lives, their needs, and the directions in which they were moving.

And yet, in another sense, Craig's love encompassed them all. Clare simply did not know this, nor did Jerome. Matthew had an inkling of it, and was in fact far closer to his father than

Clare realized. Because it was a largely unspoken closeness, it was not all that visible to Clare.

Of course, within a few days, the conversation reverted to Jerome's interest in Daniela.

'So you haven't met her yet?' Craig asked.

'I have a coffee date with her for tomorrow, darling. I'll tell you how it went afterwards, I promise. And may I invite her to dinner—if I like her, of course,' she laughed, 'with her son and Jerome, to meet you as well?'

'If you feel you have to,' he grunted, ungraciously.

'You'd be helping me, darling, if you could keep an open mind.'

'It's Jerome I'm keen to help,' he stated categorically, and Clare could see they may have a battle on their hands.

Help me, Lord, to leave this to Jerome and Craig to resolve. Help me not to take it upon myself. And she knew God would need her cooperation to realize this prayer, and she knew from experience how difficult it would be for her not to try and be the go-between.

But, Lord, be in this relationship Jerome has begun, and let it proceed only according to your wishes. Bless them all, Lord, including Luca, the young boy. Bless them, bless them all. She felt an inner nudge, to trust God, and let it rest. She was both surprised and not surprised. So swiftly had the answer come, and so clear as to her role, that she allowed herself to feel reassured and at peace.

In a lighter, brighter tone she suggested a game of cards to Craig, and over a small glass of port they sat at the dining-room table, and played a few games. Fortunately Craig won. Tempers were restored, and they enjoyed a peaceful night's sleep.

Clare looked forward with anticipation to meeting Jerome's new friend Daniela. What would she be like?

The time for Daniela to meet his mother had come but Jerome decided to leave it to the two of them to arrange. Clare asked Daniela to choose her favourite coffee shop and, not surprisingly, it was an Italian one in Constantia Village Mall—to make it convenient for Clare.

'I'll be wearing a dark blue dress, Daniela,' Clare smiled on the phone.

'And I don't know what I'll be wearing yet,' Daniela laughed, 'but I have long, dark hair.'

'Jerome has told me,' Clare responded warmly. 'We'll find each other.'

And so they did. Clare was already seated, having arrived a few minutes early, and Daniela arrived a minute early herself. Clare held out both hands, and Daniela took them into her own. They wanted to like each other, and instinctively felt it would not be difficult.

They spoke about many things—Daniela's work, Clare's sculpting and teaching, Luca and, in brief, Catholicism—the difference between the South African and the Italian variety.

Their real bond was of course Jerome, but he was a subject they dared not touch. They both had too much respect for Jerome and for each other to do so.

'I would like to invite you and Luca over to my studio one of these days, Daniela. He might be interested in some of the things he'll find there, and so might you. But I expect Jerome will bring you over sometime soon. I'll ask him to allow time for a quick tour.'

Daniela felt she had a friend in Clare, someone who was sympathetic to her situation, and who understood Jerome better than she herself did at this stage. Clare also knew what it was to be the mother of sons, and Daniela, who only had one, admired any woman who had success with her children. It seemed to take all the love, courage and diplomacy one had to raise them to become caring and responsible adults. Would she succeed with Luca? There was a saying that it took a whole community to raise a child, and she intuitively felt that she would welcome Clare being a part of that community.

By the time they parted, they each felt enriched by the presence of the other in their lives. Each gave a glowing report of their encounter to Jerome.

Before long, Nicole was due to see the haematologist for a routine visit. Matthew was concerned that things were not going as smoothly as they ought. At ten he sent Clare a text message, asking her to pray for the doctor to have clarity and competence, and for the best possible health for Nicole. She did.

Lord, guide the doctor. Enable him to make an accurate assessment. Enable him to take the appropriate steps. And, over all, Lord, bless Nicole. Bring her to full health.

Matthew prayed himself but ever since he was an infant he had trusted in his mother's prayers. When he decided to come home for lunch, Clare could see that he was distraught. Clare wanted to take him and place his head on her breast and comfort him as she had when he was a little boy, but she knew she could not do so now. Firstly, they were both standing and he was far too tall, and secondly, and most importantly, it would have been an affront to his manhood. He was trying so hard to stand on his own feet and be a support to Nicole and her family. To try and comfort him physically would have been to undermine him in some way. No, spiritual strength and emotional support would have to suffice, and that was hard enough to offer. But Clare knew faith was the key to this process.

'God already knows the outcome, darling. And he knows what's best for the two of you. Trust in him and wait with eager anticipation as he unfolds his plans . . .'

'But how can such illness and such suffering be part of his plan, Mum? How can he will it, or even allow it?'

'I can't answer that, Matthew. All I know is that he wants what is best for both of you and, if you allow him to,

71

he will bring it to pass. Trust in him even though you do not understand.'

'I'll try, Mum, I really will try. But in the meantime, what do I say to Nicole? She is hurting, she is hurting so bad—it's not just the acute discomfort of the treatment that is causing her to suffer; it's also the sense she has that God has turned his back on her, or else why would he allow this torment? And she is in torment. She is desperate. Despite the recent positive report, she now once again has no idea whether she will come through this ordeal.'

'There you can help her, darling. Give her hope. Let her know her suffering is temporary, and will give way to a greater glory—if not in this world, then in the next.'

'Oh, Mum, how can you say that? How could you? I want Nicole to live, and so does she, only without the uncertainty that's eating her alive! Will she come through this? Not knowing is almost worse than the illness at this stage.'

Clare realized she had been tactless, but it was too late now. She could not withdraw the words she had spoken—only place them in a more helpful context.

'Simply pray for her to come through this, Matthew, in the best way possible—and leave the final outcome to the Lord. None of us knows that we'll live to see tomorrow. In the meantime, I shall pray that you will both be comforted with the comfort only God knows how to give.'

Here she did embrace her son. They held each other gently for quite a while. He kissed her cheek, said 'Thanks, Mum,' and quickly left, tears glistening, and not quite steady on his feet.

Clare sat down, put her face in her hands and wept, for love of her child, and for the pain he was going through, and for Nicole.

Clare herself believed in united prayer. She and Craig prayed together daily, mainly at mealtimes, and she often enlisted the prayer support of her friends.

The whole purpose of her ecumenical group which met once a fortnight was for the communal study of Scripture and prayer. Many of the women who came had been helped by the supportive prayers of other members in the group. A colourful member was Sister Bridget whose vow of celibacy was a novelty to many of them. They appreciated her frankness and sense of humour. Once in a while they invited Father Sean along and had a home mass together—normally at Clare's house—but mostly it was the women who led and directed the activities of the group. Whether someone was celebrating a birthday or suffering a loss, sharing the joy or sorrow made the occasion more meaningful. Clare knew that before she shared Nicole's condition with the group, she needed Pam's permission to do so and, until such time as she obtained it, she would pray only in the stillness of her own heart.

Soon enough Clare heard from both Pam and Matthew that the haematologist was satisfied with Nicole's progress after all.

Thank you, Lord. She heaved a sigh of relief.

At the close of one of their meetings Sister Bridget asked when she could pay Clare a visit.

'Soon,' Clare said, without hesitation.

A few days later Sister Bridget came for tea. They were going to discuss some of the recent movements in the parish—the appointment of a new assistant priest, and the resignation of the chairwoman of the Mothers' Union. Clare alongside Sister Bridget was also involved in the catechism programme and they needed more teachers. A range of issues dear to their hearts was on the agenda.

While they were having tea and talking, Craig got home and came through the lounge to say hello on his way to his study. Clare felt her hackles rise as Sister Bridget zoned in on Craig to the exclusion of all else. Talking of global economic trends, the effect of the financial crisis on the South African market, Craig's client base, and more, drew him into her sphere where he was all but swallowed up.

Clare felt less than content. She knew she should be grateful for Sister Bridget's friendship, and she was. But she didn't like to be side-lined, and that in her own home. Soon after Craig managed to extricate himself, Sister Bridget left, blissfully unaware of having offended her friend.

Afterwards Clare discussed her feelings with Craig, which she thought was possibly a mistake, but all the same she did.

'What do you think was happening, darling? Why did I feel so side-lined?'

Craig was not the best person to ask about personal dynamics. He was skilled at the cut and thrust of the financial world, not the delicate nuances of human relations. But Clare was sufficiently rattled to need to talk about it.

'Sister Bridget is like a planet which attracts passing objects into its orbit and turns them into moons,' he rather profoundly said. 'She makes other people orbit around her. Once within her gravitational pull, they are drawn ever closer willy-nilly. She is manipulative, and if you want her in your life, you need to be aware of this and simply tolerate it.'

'Do I, darling? She is such a good friend but I wish I didn't feel so insecure . . .' Clare was surprised by the profundity of Craig's analysis.

'You need to understand how she functions if you want to keep your equilibrium around her.'

'I wish I could be more relaxed. Maybe I'm too possessive of you, darling, and jealous of your attention being on another woman, even if she is a nun!'

'Maybe you are, sweetheart. You know I am utterly devoted to you and polite to Sister Bridget only because she is your friend.'

'I need to remind myself of that when I'm next in a similar situation. There are after all a number of attractive women in our circle, and I need to be secure enough to share you with them. I know your heart is mine, and your sharing conversation and banter and laughter with them doesn't make that any less the case. But I will need to treat myself with a firm hand. Sister Bridget's obvious admiration of you, to which you responded with animation, even delight, by the way, made me feel threatened and diminished. I need to be more secure in my own worth, don't you think?'

'Yes, Clare, I do. You of all people should be secure in your own worth, and in my deep love for you. Never doubt that even when my attention is with another woman—whether nun or not—my heart and soul, my commitment, my passion belong to you alone.'

Clare felt reassured. Thoughtfully she turned her attention to her Lord.

Help me, Lord God, to rest my faith in you, to give Craig more leeway, to trust in his love for me, and in your holding us together in the palm of your hand.

She turned to her work and knew God's peace.

Along with the Wall Street Journal and the Financial Times, Craig read Shakespeare and Dickens. He liked citing them at the most inopportune moments—when family tensions were high, for example, and Clare felt more intimacy was required, not the booming voice of a distant authority, to bolster the authority Craig himself already had within the family. During Jerome's teenage years, Craig would cite Mr Micawber from *David Copperfield* at regular intervals, 'Procrastination is the thief of time. Never put off till tomorrow what you can do today.' This was when Jerome appeared to Craig to be dragging his feet doing something Craig deemed important even though it was simply that Jerome had different, teenage priorities at that moment.

There was a pervading sadness in Clare about Craig and Jerome's relationship. She would have done or given anything to make them get on better, be closer, be more intimate, but had come to believe that it was a lost cause. She had tried everything in her power and it seemed not to improve their relationship in any way. If anything, it made things worse as she got stressed and her stress rubbed off on the two of them—and, of course, on Matthew as well—and strained the atmosphere.

So she learned to value harmony instead. Accepting Craig and Jerome's lack of closeness, Clare applied her efforts to harmony in the home. Matthew benefitted. So did Craig and Jerome, and naturally, so did she. It didn't remove from her the ache she had in her heart for Jerome to have a 'real' father. He would never say so, but she knew he felt betrayed by Craig's business-like approach to life, including fathering.

Jerome in turn had a clinical streak. He had become 'manly' at an early age, and avoided sentimentality at all costs. So Clare had to be careful in how she approached him. There wasn't the easy flow of affection that she had with Matthew.

Clare often found herself wishing that Craig was more sensitive, gentler, more understanding of her and the boys' needs. She knew she was blessed to be married to a man so strong, who was such a good provider, so upright, so dependable, and so devoted to her. It seemed ungrateful even to imagine him different in any way from how he was. And these were momentary wishes, which she tried to dismiss as soon as they arose. The best she could do was put her case for greater sympathy with whichever stage the boys were at when she and Craig were alone together and usually this ended in a row rather than a rapprochement.

Each time Clare resolved not to try to influence Craig in this direction again; and almost each time the situation arose, she couldn't resist trying afresh. But these impulses stemmed largely from earlier days. The boys had become men, and needed to fight their own battles, at least in theory.

Autumn

To Autumn

Season of mists and mellow fruitfulness,
Close bosom-friend of the maturing sun;
Conspiring with him how to load and bless
With fruit the vines that round the thatch-eaves run;
To bend with apples the moss'd cottage-trees,
And fill all fruit with ripeness to the core;
To swell the gourd, and plump the hazel shells
With a sweet kernel; to set budding more,
And still more, later flowers for the bees,
Until they think warm days will never cease;
For Summer has o'erbrimm'd their clammy cells.

Who hath not seen thee oft amid thy store?
Sometimes whoever seeks abroad may find
Thee sitting careless on a granary floor,
Thy hair soft-lifted by the winnowing wind;
Or on a half-reap'd furrow sound asleep,
Drowsed with the fume of poppies, while thy hook
Spares the next swath and all its twinèd flowers:
And sometimes like a gleaner thou dost keep
Steady thy laden head across a brook;
Or by a cyder-press, with patient look,
Thou watchest the last oozings, hours by hours.

Where are the songs of Spring? Ay, where are they?
Think not of them, thou hast thy music too,—
While barrèd clouds bloom the soft-dying day
And touch the stubble-plains with rosy hue;
Then in a waiful choir the small gnats mourn
Among the river-sallows, borne aloft
Or sinking as the light wind lives or dies;
And full-grown lambs loud bleat from hilly bourn;
Hedge-crickets sing; and now with treble soft
The redbreast whistles from a garden-croft;
And gathering swallows twitter in the skies.

(John Keats, 1795-1821)

March

Thank you, Lord, that despite appearances I believe Nicole is making progress. Bless her and Matthew as he continues to support her.

And Lord, I am so excited about Jerome and Daniela. There is something so hopeful there. And Luca is such a gem. We pray for him, Lord, that what is best for his young life will come to pass. He seems to have such an implicit trust in Jerome. May he not be disappointed or hurt. Bless him, as you lead Jerome and Daniela into what is right for them too. And help me, Lord, not to think I know what that is. Help me truly to entrust the entire process to you. But bless them, dear Lord, bless them all.

Once again, Matthew was almost beside himself. Nicole was awaiting the results of her recent tests. Would she be in the clear so that life might continue with relative normality, or would she be trapped in yet another cycle of illness and possible despair?

He called Clare. There was frenzy in his voice.

'Mum, you have to pray. Go down on your knees, please, Mum, on behalf of all three of us, you, me and especially Nicole. She and I can't kneel right now, but you can on our behalf—to show God how earnest we are.'

'I will, darling, I will. But remember God sees our hearts and he knows just how earnest you both are. And I join my prayers to yours. Trust the Lord to hear us, darling, he is not deaf.'

'If you say so, Mum, I will believe it. My own faith is running low, I must admit. I will not even begin to ask why

81

Nicole has had to go through this ordeal. I have reached the stage where it is enough for me that God understands the reasons why.'

'He will honour you for that, darling. He knows your pain and perplexity and he also sees your faithfulness to Nicole. He will bless you, you'll see.'

'Thanks, Mum, I've got to go. Thanks that I have you to talk to and to pray for us. I know you will. Bye.'

Straightaway Clare went through to her bedroom and knelt at the side of her bed. It was relatively simple to pray for Matthew and Nicole. For Nicole, Clare prayed for healing, with full confidence that God could do this, and would want to. For their relationship she prayed for every blessing, and that Matthew would be strong enough to support Nicole through this difficult time. If they all could hold onto hope, and if Nicole herself especially could not give up, then there was hope indeed. Nicole's regime of intensive treatment was almost complete. Clare naturally prayed that it would be successful. What the future held for these two young people depended on this, and was in God's hands.

She picked up her Bible from the bedside table, placed it on the bed and rested her head on it. *Lord, I don't understand half of what is in your Holy Book, nor do I understand much about the deeper meaning of pain and suffering, though I know it is somehow linked to the presence of sin in the world. All I can do is bring these precious young people before you and ask you to have mercy on them. May they know your presence with them and can you bring them through this, please, dear Lord, into health and gratitude and happiness, and a strengthened faith in you?*

Clare remained on her knees for some time. Not only had she promised Matthew, she also started realizing that she needed more humility in her approach to God. This seemed a simple yet powerful way to start.

A little later, Matthew was at Nicole's bedside in her room. She was despondent. Nothing in her life hitherto had prepared her for this.

'What have I done to deserve this, Matt?' she asked.

'Nothing, dearest, nothing. This is a test, a rite of passage. It will make your faith deeper and stronger.'

'It might destroy my faith. I am in danger of losing faith in God altogether, Matt. I fear that I might.'

'No, Nicole, we won't let you. We are all praying so hard for you—your mum, my mum, and everyone else, not to mention the two of us. God is our only hope, dearest, you can't let go of his hand now, not at this critical juncture. Let him carry you. If you sink into him, you'll find that he already is carrying you.'

'I want to trust him, Matt, I really do. But it's so hard when I do not understand why he's putting me through all this suffering and trauma. I cannot explain how bad it is.'

Nicole was clearly still battling her inner demons of doubt and discouragement.

'I know, dearest—or, at least, I don't know but I have an inkling. I see you suffer, I feel some of your confusion, I am confounded by it as well. But my mum says it is not God putting you through this at all. It is the result of all the evil and sin in this world, and suffering is one way in which God continues to redeem the world through us. It can be redemptive suffering, dearest, if we let it. God is with you in it. He is not the cause or author of your suffering. He will help you through it, you will see.'

For all his eloquence Matthew was struggling to speak at all. He longed to place his head on Nicole's breast and sob, but it was inconceivable that he could turn to her for comfort at this time. He had to be strong for her, he had to be there to comfort her, to build up her wavering faith.

He held her hand in silence, stroking it gently, kissed her furrowed brow, and turned his face slightly away, so that she would not see his tears.

Finally, Nicole broke their silence. 'I feel more peaceful now, Matt. Thank you. I can sense the Lord's sweet and gentle presence again. I have been very angry with him, blaming him for my illness. I can see now that I may have misconstrued things. If your mum is right—and I remember that difficult verse in the Bible about "completing what remains of the suffering of Christ"—I can live with all of this—at least for the moment. I hope the Lord won't expect of me more than I can bear. I trust not. He is gracious indeed.'

Matthew felt the tension seep out of his body. He still wanted to cry but these would be tears of relief, and of hope. He prayed fervently for complete healing for Nicole.

He kissed her, their hearts burning with passion and breaking with tenderness.

'I'll be here first thing in the morning, best beloved. Sleep in gentle peace. The Lord is with you, remember, not against you. We are all praying for you, I most of all. You are my life. I love you.'

And he was gone. Nicole quivered with love, with relief, and now with hope.

Theirs could yet be a happy ending.

The next morning Nicole had an altogether more peaceful expression on her face—she seemed quieter, gentler, softer. Matthew needed to get to work, so couldn't afford to stay, but it was enough to encourage her and to remind her of the transition they had made the night before. She remembered only too well.

'Oh, Matt, you won't believe what a shift there's been in me. I now accept what is happening to me. The Lord impressed upon me that I need to resist the illness but not resist him. And I feel completely different about things now.'

'I am so happy to hear that, my angel. The Lord will bring us through this, you'll see, and our faith will be stronger, not weaker. And we'll know the Lord better through it all.'

'Thank you, Matt, for not giving up on me. I've been querulous and ungrateful.'

'You've been normal, dearest, but now you're in a state of supernatural grace. Let's make sure you stay there.'

'I'll do my best, Matt, I promise.'

'And God himself will sustain you and give you grace. Remember our faith is in him.'

They kissed goodbye, and he left Nicole happy, again hopeful, again thankful, so different from the despairing young woman he had encountered when he arrived at her bedside the evening before.

Matthew longed to share these developments with his mother, but he wanted to do so face to face. It would have to wait till he got home. In the meantime he texted her, 'God's grace is sufficient, Mum. Thanks for your prayers.'

While Nicole was completing the final phase of her treatment, Matthew was in a stage of transition between his parents' home and his own 'new' abode.

Matthew had rocketed into his career direction without too much soul-searching. Having completed his qualifications as a chartered accountant he found himself working at an accounting firm where he sometimes had pangs as to whether he shouldn't perhaps have followed in his mother's footsteps rather than his father's. But then he wanted to give his family a secure living one day and accounting was a surer bet in this regard. Art would have given his creative side an outlet, though, so he was almost grateful that the garden flat he had taken on was rather dilapidated and that he had carte blanche—and some financial backing from the owner—to renovate it as he saw fit.

French doors were a must. They would lighten up the place. And the bathroom needed to be accessible from the lounge and the bedroom, just in case there were visitors to stay. Matthew was eminently sociable. There was also an oak tree in the garden, with a bench underneath it, which made him feel at home. He had already sat there with his arm around Nicole. Together they chose shades of paint for the walls and new tiles for the kitchen and bathroom. It was quite a strenuous exercise but he paced it between treatments. He wanted her fingerprints on every aspect of what he was doing. This might soon be the living space for both of them, he whispered in his heart.

Barely a couple of weeks after that happy text message about the all-sufficiency of grace, Clare received a call.

'Mum, when can I bring Nicole to come and have supper with you and Dad? As soon as it suits you.' It was Matthew, sounding urgent, sounding excited. He was now spending most nights in his renovated abode.

Clare's heart beat a little faster. 'What is it, darling? Good news, I hope?'

'Just tell me when I can bring her, Mum. We'll answer all your questions when we see you.'

'Tonight, if that's not too soon for her.'

'I'll go straight to her place after work then. We'll be with you by seven. Thanks, Mum.'

Clare's heart was still beating faster than usual. She went through to Craig's study and said quietly, 'Nicole will be joining us for supper, darling.'

'Oh?' Craig seemed pleasantly surprised. 'That's an unexpected pleasure. I look forward to it.' Craig seemed to suffer from a conscientious lack of curiosity.

Only you, Lord, can keep my nerves and excitement at bay. Clare smiled to herself, grateful she had the Lord to turn to, or else she would have surely bothered her husband no end.

Seeing to supper would keep her calm. She would roast a chicken and make a fruit salad, and give thanks for Matthew and Nicole. Matthew's voice gave him away—it had to be good news.

Shortly before seven Matthew's cheery voice was at the kitchen door. 'Hello, Mum, here we are!' Before he even brushed her cheek, he held Nicole before her, standing behind his beloved, ushering her in with his hands cradling her waist.

'Look at her, Mum,' he said, proudly, as though she were his first-born child. 'How does she look to you? Doesn't she look way better?'

'Give me a chance, Matthew. Hello, Nicole,' Clare said gently, kissing her forehead, 'let me look at you.' And Clare gently placed her hands on Nicole's shoulders, looking into her smiling yet diffident eyes. 'How are you feeling, dear? And yes, Matthew, she does look way better . . . You do, Nicole.'

Nicole's eyes brightened. 'Thank you, Auntie Clare. I knew you'd only say so if it were true. I'm beginning to feel more myself again, I really am.'

'That's excellent, Nicole. How grateful we all are! Your parents must be over the moon.'

'They are, Auntie Clare. And my mum says I must say hello to you from her.'

Just then Craig entered. Soon they were all seated.

'Dad, do you have any of that non-alcoholic champagne in stock? There's something we want to celebrate, two things in fact.'

'Let me have a look.' Craig found a bottle in the corner of the big fridge. Here is some pink champagne!' With a twinkle in his eye he added, 'We don't care what the correct nomenclature is, Nicole, we call it champagne . . .'

'Whatever sounds more festive is best for us, Uncle Craig.'

'Good! So what's the occasion, Matthew? I trust we are drinking to Nicole's health?'

'Yes, first and foremost, Dad, I'd like to propose a toast to Nicole's clean bill of health. Her provisional test results came through today and we are so, so relieved and grateful. And thank you both for your prayers and support. Thanks, Mum.'

Nicole's eyes were filled with tears as they drank to her health.

'Thank you all,' she whispered, 'and thank you both for being there for me and Matthew these past months. We depended on your love and support.'

'And now another toast!' Matthew proposed a few seconds later. 'Guess!!' Matthew was so excited Clare was beginning to think along certain lines but didn't want to allow herself to. They seemed so young . . .

'You take us out of our suspense, Matthew,' said Craig, drily. 'We can see by your face this is going to be good.'

'We're getting engaged, Mum. Dad, we're engaged to be married!' Matthew's voice was trembling with emotion and Nicole's eyes were again brimming with tears of joy.

'Engaged? Am I dreaming?' Clare turned to Craig with delight. 'Tell me this is for real, Craig darling. Matthew, Nicole, congratulations!'

Deep in her heart Clare was anxious that this was too soon, that the excitement would be more than Nicole's health could bear, but she dared not whisper those fears to anyone except her Lord. A lightning prayer went up, *Bless them, precious, dearest Lord.*

'My children—because soon you will both be that—Nicole, what a lovely daughter you will make Clare and me—we wish you every joy, every success, every blessing, don't we, darling?'

Nicole's tears were infectious. Clare was all choked up.

'We do,' she managed to utter, her heart as full as could be. Her younger son was to marry his childhood sweetheart. What greater blessing could there be?

In a flash she knew what it was. *Keep her healthy, dear Lord. Keep your hand of healing upon her. Let no evil come near her. She has been through enough. Thank you, Lord,* she whispered in faith.

The rest of the evening was spent with all four of them sharing their delight.

'We'll make this official at our Easter Saturday lunch. So in the meantime, it's just for the two of you, Mum and Dad. We know our secret will be safe with you, as it is with Nicole's parents. Not even Lucy knows, neither should Jerome.'

Even long after they left, Clare's head was spinning with happiness, her prayers ever rising to God for his protection of Matthew and Nicole and their young love.

Meanwhile, in Jerome's life, things were developing slowly but surely as well. It was late one evening. Luca had gone to bed. Jerome and Daniela were seated on the couch, facing each other, each holding both the other's hands. They were looking at each other with that look love has of wanting to plumb the depths of the soul of the beloved. Each dwelt on the other with a smiling, loving gaze that wanted answers while nevertheless basking happily in the assurance of each other's love.

'What are you thinking, Jerome?' Daniela was the first to break the silence.

'About you, my love, and your beauty, and how grateful I am you and Luca have come into my life.'

'Oh, that's amazing! I was thinking the same about you. Jerome, once the dust has settled with Antonio, would you accompany me to my hometown to meet my parents and to see where I grew up?' Antonio, Daniela's ex-husband and Luca's father, had come through to Cape Town unexpectedly and been as difficult as he could possibly be, threatening her physically, and harassing Luca. He had stayed at a nearby guesthouse and come round to their apartment as often as they were home. That particular nightmare was over, at least for the moment.

'Of course I'd love to, Daniela. We could take Luca with us to visit his grandparents, and I'd love to explore Capua with you. I hope we'll enjoy some gentle strolls along the river.'

'That's something great to look forward to then,' and Daniela continued to bask in the glow of the present.

Daniela got up from the couch to go and make them coffee. Jerome inhaled the goodness of life at this moment.

Clare in the meantime had to be sure she didn't crowd them. Jerome had always needed space, and Daniela, while emotionally needy, probably didn't need Clare to be her best friend. Furthermore, Jerome confided in Clare, and if she had a relationship with Daniela which was too close, it would interfere with his freedom of mind to do so.

So Clare bided her time and treated them both with warmth and compassion. The easiest connection was in fact with Luca, who simply reached out to her in total trust and affection.

Clare reached out to Father Sean in a similar way. He was truly shepherd-like. He had a way of extending himself towards his parishioners which reminded Clare of what she herself strove for as a mother. His empathy and compassion for even the weakest among them had endeared him to her from the very start.

Jerome was more reserved in matters of faith—unless they touched on karate, when he became animated and passionate—but Matthew simply melted in the warmth of Father Sean's personality. Even Craig liked him and he, like Jerome, was not as easily pleased as she and Matthew were.

So they invited him to dinner quite regularly, and were careful not to 'match-make' him with Sister Bridget. They invited the two at the same time only when there were other guests present. Father Sean was not entirely relaxed with Sister Bridget's rather forward ways.

On one occasion Father Sean was telling them about his recent trip back home to Ireland. Sister Bridget's questions were importunate. She interrogated him on every member of his family and Clare could see him growing increasingly uncomfortable until she rescued him by turning the spotlight on Sister Bridget herself. Sister Bridget was attending classes on social work and community outreach and Clare managed to draw her out on what she found most rewarding in her new field of study. Father Sean visibly relaxed as Craig poured him another whisky. The conversation moved on and the awkward moment was no more.

'How's your work going, Clare?' Father Sean asked, always interested in what was near and dear to his parishioners.

'I'm busy with a bust, Father, interestingly enough of the apostle Peter. So I'm trying to capture the rugged features of a fisherman as well as the zeal which was surely reflected in his face. Easier said than done, I might add.'

'That sounds like quite a challenge. My mother always said that no matter what went wrong in one's life or particularly one's faith, one should look at St Peter and be encouraged. "God writes straight with crooked lines," she used to say, and in my experience he does.'

'I'll invite you to my studio to have a look at it when it's finished, Father. I'm donating it to Sister Bridget's convent for their new entrance hall.'

'Isn't that exciting, Father?' cried Sister Bridget. 'Clare is so clever.'

'That she is, Sister,' Craig muttered quietly, and they all went through to the lounge for coffee.

On this occasion Craig seemed determined not to allow himself to be hi-jacked by Sister Bridget. Clare noticed his ducking and diving with appreciation. She gently squeezed his hand as he walked past her. He knew why.

Over the years Clare had learnt to be silent, to communicate with her God in the stillness of her own heart. She suspected this was what Craig did, constantly, but he was very private on such matters, even in relation to her.

When it came to her sons, she was almost too close for comfort. It was sometimes hard to get a proper perspective and know what was best for them, and so she relinquished their respective situations to the Lord.

For Jerome she prayed for wisdom, for discernment, that he might know what was best in his relationship with Daniela. And there was of course Luca. It seemed simple enough to ask that his needs be met, the relatively uncomplicated needs of a child, although she knew that at thirteen he was hardly a child anymore and that there was in fact little uncomplicated about a teenager, but she knew intuitively that stability was good for Luca, however that may come. When it came to Daniela, she simply left her in the Lord's hands. What could she ask for? She barely knew this delicate young woman, who was beginning to lean on her son. And for Jerome himself she had always prayed for a mate who loved God and would love him. Whether Daniela was the right person for him was for Jerome to decide in the stillness of his own relationship with God. Matthew's needs at this stage seemed obvious—stabilised health for Nicole, and happiness for them both.

Clare went to bed at ten most evenings. Craig followed her at around eleven. He used that hour to catch up on the financial news of the day. She used it to read.

Presently she was reading Julian of Norwich. She found the direct simplicity of this fourteenth-century recluse refreshing and challenging at the same time. The idea of our longing for God itself being a kind of penance captured her imagination. Was there indeed a kind of suffering inherent in our lack of complete union with the divine? Or was that lack of union in fact an illusion? Only in the fullness of time would this be revealed. In our age the emphasis was on an almost automatic union, self-evident, only to be recognized. For Julian of Norwich it remained an intense yearning, realized only for moments in ecstatic visions. Clare admired rather than envied the intensity of this gifted visionary.

For herself she was grateful for the stable plane she had reached. Earlier journals showed signs of agonizing and grief as she tried to fathom the mind of God, or impress him with her petitions. She had ceased to do that now without, she hoped, becoming complacent.

Now, she believed, she rested in God, making every effort to please him but depending on his good will rather than fearing his displeasure. That he was innately pleased with us, she had become convinced of. Her realization owed a lot to her regular talks with Craig about these issues. He had a simple faith which was rock-solid, and he had an answer for everything. No mystical wonder or unresolved theological questions for Craig. Everything was clear to him, and he told Clare so in no uncertain terms. At first she had cringed at what seemed to her a lack of reverence but over time she had come to realize that there was no disrespect intended. Craig simply believed he understood these profound issues and, perhaps, with a combination of theological insight and the simple faith of a child, he did. So she had come to depend on his clarity and the strength of his conviction. She had learnt not to make him too aware of her own uncertainties as it made him impatient. He intuitively believed that his kind of faith was the proper one, and signs that Clare was deviating from total assurance disappointed him. So she kept her doubts and wonderings to herself, to share with a friend or with her Bible study group. She felt women believed slightly differently from men, tending perhaps to be less dogmatic and more searching,

It was time to go to bed. Clare felt fatigue had seeped into every cell of her body. There was nothing to do and nowhere to go except sleep. Her bed welcomed her, and she was gone.

That night she had some crazy dreams. There was one in which she was a child again and being reprimanded by her father for letting the cat out. She was cold and shivering and scared. There were to be consequences but in her dream she did not yet know what these were. She woke up shivering with cold and trembling with fear.

It was good to be awake in her own warm bed next to her strong, loving, sleeping husband. What was that dream about?

Clare tiptoed through to the kitchen to make her morning tea. She sat at the kitchen table with her head in her hands while the kettle was on.

What was that all about, dear Lord? I felt so forlorn, chastised by my father, cold, and yet I was in a warm bed next to Craig?

She then remembered that in their last conversation she had felt as though Craig was questioning her mothering style again. Instead of dreaming about him, she had transferred his authority over her as his wife to her father's authority over her as a child, and voilà, she was trembling in fear in both regards. Craig's sleeping presence beside her was the very trigger that took her into her dream of chastisement.

Yes, now I see, Lord, thank you! What shall I do with all of this?

She realized she simply needed to go about her daily tasks with a light spirit, knowing her Lord was at her side.

Clare slipped back into bed to have her first cuppa with her toes curled around Craig's. Despite their slight altercation the evening before, and despite her dream, she still had to pinch herself to realize how lucky she was to have this gorgeous man to sleep beside and wake up next to each night and day. *Help me not to lose perspective, Lord. Remind me to count my blessings. Craig loves me and he loves Jerome and Matthew. These are normal squabbles. Help me not to be oversensitive, Lord.*

Having finished her tea, she curled herself around Craig's warm body and gradually coaxed him into being awake.

Clare had a few pupils who did sculpture with her. She saw them individually as it was intensive work. Moira came once a week, on a Friday afternoon. She was the mother of three young children and found her time away from them in the calm presence of Clare a godsend.

'We might be relocating to Johannesburg,' she announced one afternoon, looking glum.

'Why, Moira? Is John being transferred?'

Moira's husband worked as a consultant for a mining company. Their headquarters were in Gauteng. Moira had often expressed to Clare how grateful she was that John was based in Cape Town.

'He's been told he might be,' she replied. 'I so hope it will work out differently but maybe it's best to be prepared for the worst.'

'Yes, the willingness to go is good but nothing stops you from praying that the door to Johannesburg closes if it's not the best thing for you and your family.'

'Really? You think I can pray like that? I don't really pray much, you know.'

'Well, now could be a good time to start,' Clare said with a smile. 'As long as you are willing to abide by John's final decision, you are perfectly entitled to ask God to work things out in the best possible way for all five of you, knowing that he already knows his plans for you, and they are plans for good and not for evil.'

'Oh, Clare, how do you know these things?'

'I read. I study. I pray. I reflect. I surrender,' Clare responded, laughing as she saw Moira's flummoxed face. 'It just needs patience and perseverance, and of course faith. Faith is the starting point.'

'How do I get it?' Moira sounded slightly desperate.

'Well, I think your current situation is a great place to begin. Simply ask God to give you faith in this dilemma to believe he has your best interests at heart—yours, John's, the children's. He knows what he's doing. Trust him.'

'I'll try, Clare, I will.'

'I'm sure you will, dear. And I'll pray for you all as well, particularly for John as he negotiates his position with the company. I'll pray that he has wisdom, and also that the managerial staff involved in this decision have wisdom. One way or another, you can rest assured it will work out for the best if you trust.'

'Thank you, Clare, I feel so much better now.'

'And one of these days, you and John must come over for a meal. You may choose if it's a lunch-time over a weekend with the kids, or a weeknight without them—whatever you and John prefer—just let me know. We'd love to have you over.'

'Oh, I know John's been wanting to meet Craig for some time now. That would be such an honour. Let's make it a weeknight without kids. Nosipho can put them to bed.'

'How's next Wednesday then?'

'Great. I'll just make sure John has nothing on and confirm with you.'

'That's fine, Moira. Let's get started.'

The clay was all ready and waiting. Moira was working on a bust of her elder son.

The evening with Moira and John approached. Clare looked forward to it. She had considered inviting Jerome and Daniela but desisted. It would then resemble a family affair, and she felt that, besides being a pleasant evening of cameraderie, the advantage would be for John to meet Craig. The tension between Jerome and Craig could easily poison the atmosphere.

So when Moira and John arrived, with a bottle of wine for Craig and a bunch of flowers for Clare, after the preliminaries were over, Clare suggested that John had a drink with Craig in his study. She and Moira would put the last touches to the preparations for dinner.

Conversation around the table was convivial. Craig had a wry sense of humour which surfaced when he was relaxed.

John had already told Craig about his possible transfer to Johannesburg so they naturally talked about it.

'So, Moira, I believe you have three young children,' Craig broached the subject. 'How do you think a move to Johannesburg would affect them?'

'Well, Clare has advised me not to worry about them but to pray about the situation, which I'm trying my best to do.'

'Clare gives good advice, Moira. And I'm sure your best is more than good enough.'

'Have some more wine, John,' said Clare.

'Remember I am to drive home,' John smiled, 'but I'll have a drop, thanks, Clare.'

'You know, when our children were small, we had to move house. A large construction firm had been asked to build a business centre in our residential block. It was traumatic for us as we were so settled,' Clare recounted.

'Clare's right,' said Craig. 'We were caught off guard, and had inadvertently taken our security from our comfortable living situation. Suddenly we faced uncertainty.'

'And so I did what I always do in a crisis—prayed for a new home, the best possible one for all of us. This is what emerged.' Clare gestured with her right arm to the lounge and with her left arm to the kitchen.

'And it is a lovely home, Clare. What happy hours even I have spent here. Did your sons adapt quickly?'

'You know, one important thing to learn as a parent is that happy parents have happy children. As long as the parents are settled happily the children take their cue from them and settle happily as well.'

John said, 'That's an important perspective to realize.'

'But surely the nature of the school and the teachers, their friends, and the parents of their friends are all factors in a child's life?' asked Moira, somewhat incredulously.

'Yes, of course they are, Moira,' Clare smiled reassuringly. 'We're just trying to say that the most important factor in a child's life is his or her home situation, so basically if you and John can reach consensus—with John's firm—on the best step, your children will adapt. And they are young. This helps. They are less attached to their friends, at this stage, and it is easier to make new ones.'

'Yes,' said Craig. 'I agree with Clare. You two focus on the big decision—to move or to stay. Thereafter you focus on the children's circumstances.'

John laughed. 'I wish we had your wisdom. It's great to have your input. That's how we're gaining wisdom, I guess.'

'We acquired it over many years,' Craig smiled like a wise old owl.

Moira helped Clare clear the table to make space for dessert. It was lemon meringue pie, Matthew's favourite. Clare wondered how he and Nicole were. Her sons were never far from her thoughts. And as often as she thought of them, she strove to pray for them.

After coffee in the lounge it was time for mutual thanks and goodbyes.

'Call me anytime, John,' said Craig, 'if you'd like to discuss anything, or just to come over for a drink.'

'Thanks, Craig. I'll do that.'

'Moira, we'll see each other on Friday, and you know you can pop round anytime between classes if you'd like to.'

'Thanks, Clare. I look forward to every Friday afternoon. We'll catch up then.'

The following week Nicole and her mother Pam came to tea. Clare anticipated that Nicole might be feeling vulnerable and self-conscious, and did her best to reassure her by at first paying attention to her mother instead. Eventually Clare drew Nicole out on her experience of the past few months since her diagnosis. She was remarkably frank. Her description of the alienation she had felt from normal life made Clare shudder.

'Contact with family and particularly Matthew were all that kept me going.'

Clare knew it would be therapeutic for her to have the chance to get it all off her chest.

'You know, Mum, and I'm sure you'll understand, Auntie Clare, how you feel when you think you might die? You feel terrified and oh, so alone. Even knowing Christ's love doesn't seem to be enough at that point, and that made me feel guilty. But the thing is I couldn't see him whereas Matthew was there, present, visible, holding my hand, kissing my forehead, smiling encouragingly, being an angel . . .'

'In fact,' said Clare gently, 'maybe Matthew was the presence of Christ himself. Matthew sometimes is that, even to those of us in his own family.'

'Oh, do you think so? I've never thought of it like that before . . .'

'And Matthew was the living presence of Christ, darling, calling you to life, not death,' said Nicole's mother, warming to this view of things.

Nicole sat quietly, pondering their words, seeing her beloved in a new light, one which suffused her soul as she accepted its validity. How blessed she was . . . She should revel in this realization and move away from meditating on the evils of her recent past. She longed to move forward, with Matthew, and his mother's gentle presence served only to reassure her.

By the time they left, they had covered Nicole's studies, her diet and exercise plan, and her love of birds. She had an aviary at home and her eyes shone brightly as she described her birds and their ways.

'Mum, can Auntie Clare come and have tea with us next time? I want to show her my winged treasures!'

'Of course she can, Nicole. At Bible study we'll discuss a suitable time. Maybe Matthew could come along as well.'

'Oh, no, Mum, this first time I want it to be us three women only. Then I can entertain Matthew when I tell him about it. He'd love me also to have a life of my own—I'm way too dependent on him!'

'What a wise young lady,' said Clare, smiling. 'I look forward to meeting your lovely birds soon. Thanks for coming over and sharing your recent experience, Nicole. I know it must have been painful, but it helps to get it out into the open, and now you can move on.'

'Yes, I know. Thanks, Auntie Clare.'

Clare kissed her gently on the forehead.

They left, and Clare walked slowly back to the house. *She is so young, Lord*, she mused. *Why did she have to suffer like that? Do you ever tell us, Lord?*

She sensed the Lord's gentle chiding, reminding her that he knew best for his children, and that no one was more loved than Nicole, with her gentle, trusting spirit. She and Matthew had been refined as by fire, and would be blessed beyond their wildest dreams.

I shall trust you, Lord, and not make myself anxious over your ways, your plans, your designs. I shall simply entrust my loved ones to you. Clare was soothed, comforted with the very comfort she had bestowed on Nicole. She sat quietly at the kitchen table, prayerfully, waiting for Craig to come home.

When Clare did eventually visit Pam and Nicole, she had a delightful time. Not only was she a bird lover herself, but she also enjoyed inhabiting a young woman's world, having no daughters of her own.

'Your birds are beautiful, Nicole. So is your room—just like you. It's been an honour to get to spend time with you here in your neck of the woods. Now I know why Matthew cannot stay away from you for long!'

She resolved to step up her daily prayers for Nicole's well-being and prayed for every blessing on her and Matthew's relationship. They were a pleasure to pray for. It made her feel buoyant and light.

April

The autumn leaves are beautiful, crisp and golden brown in the sun. Thank you, Lord, that Nicole is through the worst. Now she and Matthew can move forward with their lives. Bless them, dear Lord, and heal them both. They have been so shattered by this devastating experience. May they once more believe in the goodness of the life you have created.

Lord, I do believe this Easter could be a very special time. Commemorating our wedding anniversary and Matthew's baptism on Easter Saturday always makes it a blessed day, but this year we have the added joy of Nicole's healing and the announcement of her and Matthew's engagement. Bless her whole family as they join us for this occasion.

'**M**um, I'd like to have coffee with you sometime soon.' It was Jerome's somewhat gruff and husky voice on the phone. 'I need to get your angle on something. When can we make it?'

Clare knew Jerome would only do this under urgent circumstances, urgent to him, of course. And she suspected this could only pertain to Daniela or maybe Luca.

'You could pop home this afternoon, Jerome, or we could meet for a coffee wherever you like tomorrow morning.'

'Will Dad be home this afternoon?'

'Probably, darling, but we could have our coffee in the studio, if you like. That way we'd have maximum privacy. Dad will understand and he won't disturb us. What time would you be able to come? I'll be there and waiting.'

'Three'ish, Mum. Thanks. See you then. Love you,' Jerome couldn't resist adding. Occasionally he was struck by the realization of how lucky he was to have her in his life, almost always affirming him, loving him and, in a sense, although he had to share her, belonging to him. He already felt better, simply having made the call.

Seated in the nook where Clare had a comfortable couch, armchair and coffee table, each with a mug in their hand, Jerome launched into the issue troubling him.

'It's Luca's father, Antonio, Mum. He's making late-night, threatening calls from Italy now, harassing not just Daniela, who's learning to be strong, but Luca. I don't understand him. Mum! Why would he want to make his own child miserable?'

'He's struggling to let go, darling. Imagine losing a son as gentle and precious as Luca. It must be hard. Besides, he doesn't seem to be a particularly rational person, to put it mildly.'

'No, he definitely isn't. He's unreasonable and malicious, accusing Daniela of betraying him, when they've been divorced for two years already. What am I to do about him, Mum? The most vicious karate chop would barely suffice but he's miles away in Naples and has practised long-distance sorcery on both of them. What shall I do?'

'Well, Jerome, my advice to you would be to stay strong and steady. Both Daniela and Luca need someone they can depend on, and you now are that person. If you allow yourself to get rattled then they will be surrounded by stormy waves. If you, on the other hand, are able to remain rational and responsible, there is security for them in you. Let Daniela experience the strong and resolved you—at this point, anyway—when

Antonio is causing tumultuous waves. That helps her to be strong for Luca.'

'I am also worried about Luca, Mum. He is so vulnerable. He is such a nice kid, and it eats him up alive to know his father is suffering. At the same time, he is fiercely loyal to me—it is so touching—not just through karate, but also because he can see Daniela is really happy with me. The poor boy is torn between us three adults, and he doesn't know how to deal with his father's calls, tantrums, demands and, frankly, sophisticated spying techniques. What shall I tell Luca? How shall I handle him at this stage? I don't want him to feel he has to choose between me and his father . . .'

'No, of course you don't, darling. I don't want to interfere but you know Luca and I get on rather well, and if you and Daniela would allow him the opportunity to chat with me and Dad—who also likes him a lot—or even to spend a night or two here, it might give him a chance to get some of what is bothering him off his chest and to gain some perspective. He's most welcome. No pressure but maybe discuss it with Daniela and Luca and see what they think. It may just take the heat off him, and Antonio doesn't have our phone number.' They both smiled.

'Thanks, Mum, that's a great idea. He'd probably love to get away from the intensity of it all and spend some boyhood time here, in my old room, which seems to charm him.'

'Yes, he loves it! He idolizes you, Jerome. Okay, then, you let me know. Anytime is fine with us.'

Jerome left, after somewhat cursorily greeting Craig, rather happy with this new plan. He was eager to hear what Daniela thought of it. He knew he needed to keep her fully in the loop. The last thing she needed was to feel marginalized by him and his mother, but Clare would see to it that she didn't. He knew he could trust his mother on this one.

Clare longed to draw alongside Daniela and befriend her, woman to woman, but she dared not do more than she already had done. Jerome should not feel he was having a relationship with his mother's friend. No, she was to remain Jerome's mother, first and foremost, and only secondly, a womanly support to Daniela. Craig had made this perfectly clear to her. She was too close to the situation to have recognized its perils herself, and the very last thing she wanted to do was to destabilise their still fragile relationship—fragile because of the wave-tossed sea surrounding them in the form of desperate and dangerous Antonio.

The courts in Italy had a firm grip on him as there was a restraining order against him but this had not yet translated into his being under proper legal authority when in South Africa. Here he seemed free to terrorise them at will and Jerome felt the weight of responsibility fall heavily upon his shoulders. He thanked God daily for his background in karate and the skills and ethos it had taught him. It made him feel so much less vulnerable and in a much better position to protect Daniela and Luca—at least physically—but he knew they were at great risk emotionally. This was especially true of Luca, with the natural love he still had for his father, and torn between Antonio, on the one hand, pressurizing and bullying him, and his loyalty to his mother and Jerome, on the other. There were no easy solutions.

'If only Antonio could fall in love with someone else,' Daniela would wistfully say at times.

'Oh, Mama, don't say that,' Luca would cry. 'Then I'd have a stepmother and I would hate that.'

'You might not, Luca. She might be nice.'

'Don't even think about it, Mama. Please stop!'

Jerome would laughingly intervene, just to lighten the situation.

'I think both of you need to leave Antonio to conduct his own love life. The important thing here is that we prevent him from terrorising you two, and I take it as my job to achieve that. So let's go to Kirstenbosch Gardens for a walk and for tea, and let's put this matter out of our minds as far as possible, otherwise we give Antonio the victory. And, Luca, while it is good that you love and respect your father, it is not good that he spoils your life from afar, so try to be strong and live your life independently of him. Through his threats and violence he has given up all authority over you—I am sad to utter such harsh words but it is true—so it is best for you to become self-reliant with your mother and me always alongside you to guide and advise you. And let karate make you strong. It has already begun to do so.'

'Thanks, Jerome. I know what you say makes sense. It is still very hard for me because he's my father, after all. But I've become scared of him.'

'Your mother and I will protect you, Luca.'

'Yes, Luca, we want you to trust us and always tell us what's going on and how you feel. Will you do that?'

'I'll try, Mama. I really will.'

By now they were on their walk and Luca was building up an appetite for the tea and scones he had developed a liking for. They started talking about other things, Luca's approaching birthday party, his school-friends, his teachers, and very soon he had a sparkle in his eyes and his boyhood glow had returned.

Oh, Lord, protect him, Daniela prayed, *and let our cries come before your loving throne of mercy and grace. Protect my child, and protect me and Jerome too. Protect Antonio from himself, and lead him away from us, dear Lord.*

At tea Daniela drew her chair closer to Jerome's.

'With the two of you, I am content and at peace,' she whispered. 'Both of you, please, stay close by my side.'

'We will,' they replied in unison, 'we will.'

Daniela laughed with childlike joy, resting her head on Jerome's shoulder.

Luca looked satisfied as he finished off his milkshake, an additional treat, and he could see how content his mother was with the man who had become far more than his karate coach.

By the time they left, all three of them had renewed strength. Jerome dropped them off and then went to his place to continue studying for a major test he had the next day.

In the meantime Clare's student Moira gave her an urgent call. She sounded distraught.

'Why don't you come over for tea, Moira? I'll put the kettle on.'

Moira arrived looking washed out and miserable. Clare knew immediately that something serious was wrong.

'What is it?' she asked, concerned.

'I don't want to be disloyal, Clare, but I have to talk to someone wiser than me, and you're the safest person I know.

'What is it, Moira? Please tell me. You know you can trust me with anything.'

'It's John. He's been gambling. Your husband would kill him if he knew. When we were here for supper they did apparently discuss the pros—if there are any—and cons of gambling and Craig persuaded John not to touch it. He told him it was a very dangerous habit and could lead to our ruin. John said he understood.'

'And now what?'

'Now he's gone and used all our credit cards to the max, and lost all that it was possible to lose on them. Thank God we still have our house and cars, and the few investments Craig recently made for us. But John—or I—or you, dear Clare—will have to tell Craig that we need to cash them in so as to settle all the ghastly credit card debt which John has run up in less than two weeks. How could he? I have to struggle with myself not to despise him totally. He promised me—and Craig—that he would never gamble again. I can't trust him at all, can I?'

Clare was silent. What could she say that would be helpful?

Moira continued.

'I am so furious. I don't trust myself to speak to him at all. I am sure I'll regret whatever words may come tumbling out of my mouth. Ever since the bank called, I've alternated between being absolutely livid and then tearful. Could you maybe call him, Clare? It is just a thought I now have. Could you call him, just to tell him where I am, and to make sure he gets home to the kids, or arranges with Nosipho to stay late? I dare not speak to him.'

'Let's talk first,' Clare said, laying her hand on Moira's shoulder. 'Could you speak to Nosipho yourself, just to check whether she can stay longer with the kids, and then we deal with John in a little while, when you're not so upset?'

Moira heaved a heavy sigh of discouragement.

'Okay, I can do that.' She called Nosipho, spoke to her briefly, and hung up. She started crying.

'Why did he do this?' she asked, distraught, perplexed, and angry. 'Do you understand why he did this, Clare? Please help me. I am so furious I feel as though I never want to see him again. Is he a gambling addict, do you think?'

'I don't know much about addiction, Moira, perhaps Craig would know better about gambling and its causes. I think he's had to deal with this problem before. Once you're calmer, I think it might be a good idea to consult him, or, better still, to persuade John to consult with him, man to man, as it were. The positive thing is that they've already broached the subject before. Also, that way, John won't feel that we women are ganging up on him. What do you think of that idea?'

'Oh, Clare, I knew you would help me! Maybe that *is* a good idea. One thing I'm sure of and that is that under the present circumstances I cannot stay in the same house as John tonight.'

'You can always sleep over here, Moira, but I don't think that is ideal. Why should you be away from your home and children because of something John has done? He should rather stay elsewhere. But best case scenario is that you and John resolve things tonight with my and Craig's help. I'm going to make you a fresh pot of tea and go and consult with Craig quietly by myself while you enjoy the fragrance of the jasmine I will pick you in the garden. Do your best to relax and to trust that this matter will be resolved.'

Clare and Craig spoke. John was invited round. And, most importantly of all, John and Moira were able to speak to each other without screaming.

'You know where to find us,' Clare said as the couple left in their separate cars. Craig put his arm around Clare's waist and drew her gently towards him.

'No wonder your students love you,' he said. 'No wonder they do. And I love you too.' He kissed her on the forehead, and hand in hand they walked towards the house, knowing their marriage was a precious treasure, one to be nurtured and valued.

In moments like these, Clare knew she had the best husband in the world.

However, each interaction she had with her elder son reminded her that his sense of his father was altogether different from hers. Jerome felt disgruntled. Why did his father always make him feel humiliated? It was as though Craig revelled in his discomfort. Approaching his father on any matter almost always caused him pain.

His mother was so different. She was a peach, smooth and gentle, cooperative and giving. But right now he wanted to try and puzzle out his relationship with his father.

His mother of course was crucial to this relationship as she was most often the go-between. Could this be part of the problem? he found himself wondering. Perhaps he should take a more direct line of approach and courageously approach his father man to man . . .

'Dad's stodgy, Mum,' Jerome said.

Clare went very silent, very still. *Does he not know it's not permissible for him to criticize Craig to my face?* Yet at the same time she wanted him to feel free to unburden himself. If he could not speak honestly to her about his feelings towards his father, to whom could he? *Well, there's Matthew, and now there's Daniela,* she reasoned. *But I like to be confided in,* she realized, *even though I know I need to be loyal to Craig.* Above all, she knew there was an element of truth in his observation. She tried not to be critical herself.

'Is that how you feel, Jerome? I hope it no longer affects you.'

'Not much, but it affects you, and that bothers me.'

Jerome had not lost his protectiveness towards Clare, and deep down she hoped he never would.

'Don't worry about me, darling,' she reassured him. 'I've adapted to all facets of Dad's character.'

Have I done enough, Lord, to enable bonding between Jerome and his father? Have I over-parented, and given Craig too little space with his sons? Clare was occasionally attacked by bouts of self-doubt, and tried not to become depressed. When she had the presence of mind to pray during these times, she normally ended up by feeling pacified, forgiven, understood, but it did not prevent an attack of doubt, self-questioning, and nerves at a later stage.

And now, there was Matthew, with the trauma he had recently experienced. What a concern, what an anxiety! And yet, typically, a sweetness of spirit prevailed in all her dealings with both Matthew and Nicole, extended now to Nicole's mother Pam. They shared a gentleness which was like a sweet fragrance pervading the atmosphere they breathed. She was immeasurably thankful for this, and touched by it.

Jerome and Daniela were different. Daniela was so intense, and Jerome at times abrasive. Yet she was gradually learning to accept that, despite her initial misgivings, they seemed to be good for each other.

But Antonio's renewed presence in the country was certainly not good for any of them.

When Jerome called her to ask whether Luca could come and stay, she could detect the anxiety in his voice.

Tears were streaming down Luca's face as he walked into the kitchen with Jerome.

'Oh, Luca, I'm sorry,' said Clare, taking him by both hands to the seat right next to hers at the table. 'Can I get you a hot mug of milo?'

'Thank you, Auntie Clare.' There was a stifled sob but then his shoulders began to relax.

'Do you want to tell me what happened?' Clare asked, putting the milo beside him, 'or do you just want to relax and talk later?'

'I don't want to think about anything right now, Auntie Clare. Sometimes I just hate my father.'

'I understand, Luca, I do understand.'

Jerome made himself coffee and offered Clare a cup of tea.

'Thanks, darling,' she responded. 'I'm very glad you thought of bringing Luca here. Luca, Jerome's old room is ready and waiting for you—at any time—do you have any things with you?'

'No, Auntie Clare, but Jerome said I can just tell him what I need and he'll fetch it.'

'That sounds like a good plan.'

'Mum, I have a karate class coming up in half an hour. Can I leave Luca with you and then I'll check in with his stuff later this afternoon. Just send me a text message with a short list of what you need for the next few days, Luca.'

'Thanks, Jerome, I will.' Luca was looking far more relaxed though not yet untroubled.

'You go through to your room, Luca,' Clare said reassuringly, 'and I'll follow you there shortly.'

Jerome gave Luca a squeeze around his shoulders and walked with his mother to his car. 'Thanks, Mum, you're a gem.'

'Luca is welcome here anytime. Jerome, I'm glad you know that. I'm sorry the situation with Antonio is so messy. Would you like to tell me what happened?'

'Antonio pretends to be paying Luca a fatherly visit, takes him out and then tries to find out from him the most intimate details of my and Daniela's relationship. Luca is so loyal to us but his father threatens to beat him if he doesn't talk, and believe me actions will soon follow words.'

'Oh, how awful for all of you. How is Daniela?'

'Maybe she'll accompany me later, Mum, then you'll see for yourself. I've got to go,' and he kissed her lightly on the lips and was gone.

Despite the tawdriness of the situation, her heart swelled with pride. He was a man in every sense of the term. He was protecting his woman and her son. If ever she was grateful that he'd learnt karate, now was such a time.

Daniela and Jerome arrived in time for supper. She looked pale and drawn but put on a brave face.

'Thank you, Clare, for having Luca to stay,' she said while Luca was still in his room. 'We all so appreciate it.' Clare noticed how she was speaking on behalf of this family of three that they had begun to form.

'It's always a pleasure to have Luca and he's welcome anytime.' By now Luca had joined them and he was struggling to fight back the tears as he saw his mother.

'Has he left yet, Mama? When is he going?'

'I'm trying to encourage him to take an earlier flight, Luca, but I don't know whether he'll listen to me.'

'Stay away from him, Mama, please do, he may kill you.' Luca was verging on hysteria and Clare sat him down between her own seat and Daniela's and opposite Jerome.

'You are safe here, Luca, and your mum is safe with Jerome. Let us pray that your father won't harm anyone, including himself. Let us eat now.'

Luca moved close to his mother and looked pleadingly at Jerome. 'You'll protect Mama, won't you, Jerome?' he asked.

'Of course I will, Luca. Don't worry about that. Remember, I'm your sensei,' and he smiled.

Luca was pacified but not fully reassured. The temperamental and violent nature of his father he knew only too well for comfort. He shuddered as he attempted to settle down and eat his food.

When dinner was over Jerome suggested to Daniela that she spend some time with Luca alone in his room. She took up his suggestion, and they left the others.

Once Jerome was alone with his parents, he placed his head in his hands and looked even more troubled than Luca had done.

'This man seems desperate.' He addressed himself to both of them but predominantly to his father. 'Dad, what do you suggest I do?'

'Son, I suggest you arrange a restraining order which covers South Africa in addition to the one already in place in Italy. Although Daniela has only been here for a couple of years, such a restraining order might be easier to obtain as there is already one in place in Italy. Your old school-friend Martin might be a good person to consult.'

'Oh, would he? Thanks, Dad, I'll give him a call on Monday.'

Daniela returned, having left Luca in Jerome's old room with his laptop and all its entertainment potential on the desk.

She felt deep gratitude towards Clare and Craig for welcoming her son into their home.

'Thanks again, dear Clare and Craig. We shall come round tomorrow again if you don't mind.'

'Of course we don't, Daniela. Come anytime.'

'We'll call you in the morning, Mum, and speak to Luca, and take it from there. We're both going to stay at my place till Antonio's gone. He hasn't managed to locate it thus far, and if he does, I may have to resort to a karate move or two.'

'Be careful. Goodnight, Jerome. Goodnight, Daniela. All shall be well, you'll see.'

All shall be well, and all manner of things shall be well, and the rose and the fire are one. This was Clare's adaptation of Julian of Norwich's affirmation. And right now Daniela was the rose, and Jerome the fire. Harmony would be restored, of that she was convinced.

A couple of weeks later, when the dust had settled and Antonio was back in Italy, Jerome called while Clare and Craig were enjoying a peaceful supper.

'Sorry, Mum, to disturb your supper. Just wanted to speak to Dad about something.'

This was unusual. And Clare was tentatively happy. Anything that strengthened the bond in a positive way always gave her hope.

'Dad, Daniela has inherited some money in Italy and wants to know how best to deal with it. Can you advise her?'

'Of course, son, I'd be only too happy to do so. We can make an appointment right away.'

'Son,' Clare inwardly repeated to herself. 'Son . . .' She could probably count on one hand the number of times she had previously heard Craig call Jerome thus but these days it seemed to be a regular occurrence.

And suddenly it struck her. There was now another woman at the centre of Jerome's life, and Craig no longer resented, or felt threatened by, his son's relationship with Clare. She had given her children the best possible attention; indeed, perhaps sometimes to the detriment of her husband. Could she have contributed to the strained relationship between Craig and Jerome? It always seemed worse when she was present. Man to boy and now man to man they seemed to get on with a greater degree of ease.

'Leave Luca with me,' Clare said the next evening, having invited Jerome and Daniela to stay for supper after their consultation with Craig.

Luca had brought some homework along.

'Is there anything you think I could help you with, Luca?' asked Clare. 'My strengths are languages. What do you study besides English?'

'I do Italian privately, and French at school, Auntie Clare.'

'I tell you what . . . I'll get you a drink while you sit at Jerome's old desk or at the kitchen table, whichever you prefer, and study. Just ask if you think I can be of any use to you at all. I do know French but your Italian is definitely better than mine!'

Luca laughed, and opted to sit at Jerome's old desk.

Jerome came in ahead of Craig and Daniela.

'I've left them to complete the paperwork by themselves,' he said, 'to give me a few minutes with my favourite mama.'

'How're things going, darling?' Clare asked quickly. Luca was still at his desk so these were a few precious moments that she had Jerome to herself.

'Things are going well, thanks, Mum. Really well. Daniela is so different from all the preconceptions I had . . . Well, I guess she's so different from you, Mum. None of that serenity. All drama and intensity instead. But I love her without doubt. She makes me feel like a real, strong man, like Dad, I guess.'

'I'm so happy for you, Jerome. And it's so great that you're using Dad as her consultant. I can see it means a lot to him.'

Daniela and Craig came through to the kitchen. Daniela looked relieved, Craig charmed. There was something in the vulnerability of this slender Italian beauty that touched him. Both Clare and Jerome were delighted.

Once they were all seated in the dining-room, it rested on Clare's shoulders—and a delightful burden it was—to ensure that everyone was comfortable and at ease. She kept an eye on Luca, as so often the case he was the only teenager among adults, and watched with delight the enchanted trio of Craig, Jerome and Daniela exchanging banter. Suddenly she was even more grateful for Daniela's presence in Jerome's life. Could she be the answer to prayer in more ways than one? *Thank you, Lord,* Clare whispered, inaudibly, *that Craig and Jerome, for once, are at peace. Bless this beautiful woman and her son. May they find a comfortable place in our family.* She dished up the main course for everyone and passed the side dishes around, again keeping a watchful eye on Luca, and grateful beyond expression for the light atmosphere bathing the other three. *I'd almost given up, Lord. I'm so sorry.* Clare knew God's forgiving touch, and allowed herself to be drawn into the conversation.

Finally Easter Saturday dawned. It was a mellow day. The oak leaves were tinged with brown and the mature sun infused the earth with a deep and comforting warmth.

Clare knew lunch would go well. She had asked Elsa to come in for the morning, just to help get everything ready before the guests started arriving. Grannie Mac wasn't invited to this one. Clare didn't trust her to be discreet around Nicole and her family. But she had called in the morning to wish Clare and Craig a happy anniversary. They appreciated her thoughtfulness.

The guests consisted largely of Nicole's family and some old friends of the MacMillans and the Haydens. They were given fruit punch or champagne on arrival and after some general chitchat took their seats. A Greek salad starter followed by chicken casserole and cheesecake contributed to the pleasant yet nevertheless subdued atmosphere. Nicole and Matthew sat quietly side by side seemingly in a world of their own. Nicole's father knew almost no one outside of his own family but he made an effort to be sociable. He and Jerome got involved in a conversation about karate.

After Craig's regular short speech in which he proposed a toast to his 'loving and faithful wife' and to Matthew, his 'beloved son, dedicated to Christ on this day so many years ago', it was Matthew's turn. Matthew also made a short speech, announcing his and Nicole's engagement, to the delight of those present who weren't already in the know.

'The next time this particular group are gathered together, I trust it will be at our wedding.' And he produced Nicole's engagement ring that she had not yet started wearing in public. There were more toasts all round.

Once the guests started mingling again, Daniela found herself all alone, as Jerome and Nicole's father were moving ever deeper into the philosophy and ethos of karate.

As he watched her, Matthew felt increasingly protective towards Daniela. Was he projecting Nicole's vulnerability onto her? Or—more strangely still—did he underestimate his brother's capacity for sympathy and understanding? Perhaps in fact he was simply responding to the innate qualities of Daniela herself. She combined emotional intensity and her own particular vulnerability. It was natural for a man to want to put his arms around her.

The camaraderie between the brothers remained unaffected by the interplay between themselves and their womenfolk. The stakes could never be as high as they were when they were growing up in the presence of the same mother. She had to be a wizard of discerning whose needs were more urgent at any given time. She judged by counterbalancing instinct and intelligence. When she observed them now as young adults, she trusted that she had been reasonably successful.

Matthew's conversations with Luca were about computer games and football. Matthew followed one or two English teams but had a superficial knowledge of Luca's favourite Italian teams. This made Luca glow with enthusiasm.

'Do you think that you, Jerome and I could go to a football match together, Matt? That would be so cool . . .' Luca had a friend at school called Matthew so had devised his own way of differentiating them, and he'd quickly picked up on Nicole's term of endearment.

'I'll speak to Jerome, Luca, or maybe you should, and we'll see what we can do. Let's see if we can get it together for next weekend.'

'Oh, thanks, Matt, gee, that would be awesome!' and Luca glowed with anticipation.

Daniela joined them and, after chatting for a while, Matthew left in search of Nicole. She was sitting at the kitchen table, looking weak, and talking to Clare.

'Shall I leave you two alone? Mum? Nicole? Am I disturbing you?'

'No, join us, Matthew. Nicole needs your support.'

'Of course, I know she does. Is anything wrong?'

'Everything's wrong, Matthew. You know it is.' Nicole sounded agitated.

'I know, my love, but has anything particular happened now to upset you?'

'It's only that you seem to spend an inordinate amount of time talking to Daniela and her son.'

'Sorry, my love, it was not meant to offend you. I'm getting to know them, for Jerome's sake. And they're different from us, they're Italian, and intense, and might be oversensitive if one ignored them. I'm trying to do a balancing act here, and maybe I'm not succeeding.'

Clare left the kitchen on the pretext of fetching something from her bedroom.

When she returned, Matthew was sitting beside Nicole with her head on his shoulder.

'I'll leave the two of you,' she said.

Tears were running down Nicole's face. Why was she being so unreasonable? She knew the reason, and she knew Matthew understood it, but it made her feel no less vulnerable—in fact, if anything, even more so. She felt she had been in a dark tunnel, built with bricks of nightmare. Matthew could stand at the entrance and at the exit, but he could not get in there with her, nor could her mother or Clare. They could sympathize with her but not share her experience of hell. She felt dehumanized, and found it so difficult to believe that Matthew was still attracted to her, as he had been since they were in their mid-teens.

Why would he love a dying woman? Because despite the positive prognosis, that's what she still sometimes felt she was, so deeply had she imbibed the dangers of her illness.

But Matthew saw her inner beauty, beneath the still palpable effects of her recent treatment. And he now had great hope, thanks to his earnest conversations with her medical team, and of course his mother. He prayed that he could instil this assurance in Nicole herself. Should she not heed the positive message coming from her medical team, as he had done? Especially on this happy occasion?

But he knew that after the trauma of the past few months this was easier said than done. Expecting the worst had become a habit it was difficult to break. Nevertheless, he would persevere in trying to get her to remain positive and not just to visit this state of mind for a short spell. In time she would come round to being confident once more, and not be threatened by another woman in a most uncharacteristic way. In the meantime he needed to appreciate how fragile she was despite her clean bill of health, despite their engagement. Her feelings still needed to catch up with the facts.

The following week Luca was spending the last weekend in April at a friend's house. Jerome and Daniela decided to go for a walk in Newlands Forest and afterwards to have supper out.

Halfway through the walk, they sat down on a bench. After a few moments of relaxed silence, Jerome leant forward, cupped both her hands in his, and said, 'Daniela, I hope you're ready for this.'

'For what, Jerome? Whatever it is, I'll try to be,' with a faint smile.

'Will you marry me, Daniela, and let me love and protect you forever?'

'Oh, Jerome,' and she inhaled sharply, a sob catching in her voice. 'Goodness, this is sudden. It is what I so hoped for and yet it has completely taken me by surprise! Of course, the answer is yes. How could I possibly resist you? Such an offer to myself—and Luca. Yes, Jerome, yes!'

'And, speaking of Luca, we'll have children together as well, won't we, Daniela, in the future?'

'Of course we may, Jerome. But please let's not stress about that now. One at a time is enough. For now we have Luca.'

'And I love him as I would my own children, Daniela, I surely do. But let's keep an open mind as to the future . . .'

'Oh, Jerome, you want to marry me! And I've accepted! That is enough of a miracle for now, and almost more than I can take in. Let's have a quick meal, and then go home so that we can be alone together.'

By the time they reached Daniela's apartment, she was calmer and more confident with the new state of things. She made coffee and they also opened the bottle of champagne Jerome had sneaked into the back of the fridge to celebrate. But first they embraced.

Tenderness, passion, joy, and hope all characterized that long and silent embrace. They were each filled with their own unspoken fears and desires, some too deep even to mention to the other. Jerome now realized that even his very natural desire to have children with his future wife was not self-evident to her. He would need to tread very gently. No doubt he would talk to his mother about it. She was the most confidential person he knew and he also knew she would see both sides of the situation. She was a woman, she liked Daniela and would most certainly embrace her as a daughter-in-law, and she would bring her wisdom to bear on the intensity of Jerome's feelings. He guessed Daniela would bare her soul to her parish priest. Although he sometimes felt slightly jealous of her closeness to him, he was predominantly grateful that she had his wisdom and solicitude to depend on.

Between Jerome and Daniela themselves at this moment, however, all was sweetness and light.

When Luca got home on the Sunday evening, they needed to break the happy news to him. They both knew he'd be more than delighted.

'Would you like to tell him alone, Daniela?' Jerome asked.

'No, Jerome, I'd far rather you were present. You are the tangible reward of our decision, and he'd love to have you present when he learns the news.'

'Okay, then I'll stay.'

Luca was over the moon, more exuberant even than Daniela had been at Jerome's proposal. He had no demands or expectations to contend with. There was simply the pure joy of having Jerome permanently in his life to shield his mother from more trauma and pain and to protect him from his natural father, who had become a monster.

'Jerome, may I call you "Dad"?'

'If you'd like to, you certainly may, although I'm quite young to be the dad of a strapping lad like you!' and Jerome ruffled his hair.

'We'll talk about time frames tomorrow, Daniela. Go to work, feel normal, or rather, experience the "new normal", and let me bring over some pizza for us all to celebrate together. Then while Luca is doing his homework, you and I can discuss our arrangements.'

'That'll be fine, Jerome. Let's do that. See you tomorrow then.'

And they had a longer-than-usual, silent embrace again.

For the rest of the evening Daniela and Luca couldn't stop smiling. Jerome too went to sleep happy. Confident as he had been, it was different—and joyful—to have proposed and been accepted.

Monday evening arrived. There was pizza, non-alcoholic sparkling 'wine', and much joy and hilarity.

The snake in the grass was Antonio. Even though he was living in Naples, his influence was palpable. He would have to be told, or would he? Luca's situation would be different from previously—he would have a stepfather—and common courtesy denoted that Antonio should know about this. But, with someone so violent and so frequently drunk, was it necessarily wise to observe the rules of common courtesy? Had he forfeited his right to know?

Jerome, Daniela and Luca put their heads together on this one, and it was Luca who ruled the day.

'I want Antonio to know that Jerome is my stepdad. It will make him jealous and angry but he will have to treat Jerome with more respect. And Jerome is very important in my life, and Antonio must know this.'

Both Daniela and Jerome were impressed by the quiet authority with which Luca spoke.

'If that is your wish, Luca, we will respect it. Do you want me to tell your father, or do you want to do it yourself?'

'No, Mama, I would prefer it if you did it please. I know he'll be furious but I think it's better if the anger is between the two of you.'

Daniela immediately realized she had expected too much of Luca, and was sorry, but glad—and proud—that he could articulate his position so clearly.

'I'll write him a letter, Luca, and send it to the lawyer's office. In that way he can learn of it in a formal manner and know that his reaction will be monitored by the lawyers, just as his behaviour to us now is under surveillance since the new restraining order came through.'

'Oh, Mama, that sounds so horrid.'

'It is, Luca, but we need to do it like this to protect ourselves, you included. Antonio won't be happy that there is another man in your life, acting as your father in many ways, and we don't want you to become the victim of his violent ways. So let it be so this time. I do believe it's the only realistic way to break the news to him.'

'Okay, Mama, if that's what you think.'

'And I agree with your mother, Luca. We need to protect both you and her, and it is not only the lawyers who will do this. I also will. You'll see.'

Luca went to bed that night scared, yet reassured, grateful that he was so many miles away from Italy. He felt safe with Jerome and trusted that in time he would feel safer still. And he was so, so happy for his mother. She had found a loving man to share her life with. It certainly took the pressure off him and allowed him the freedom to be a normal and almost carefree boy, with the enticements of his teenage years stretching out before him.

Craig's reaction was less gracious. 'I'm not happy that Jerome has gone and engaged himself to this Italian divorcée—that I'm not—as charming as she may be. Marrying her would be a massive complication to his young life, and totally unnecessary.'

'Unless he loves her, darling, and then it might appear entirely necessary to both of them.'

'And even to you, by the sound of it . . .'

'Yes, darling, even to me. I like Daniela, and I think she makes Jerome happy. She is also a complex person, with plenty of life experience to make her understanding and compassionate, and they might just be right for each other.'

'And then there's her son, Luca, a teenager—what can Jerome know about raising a teenager?'

'What you taught him, when you raised him and Matthew. He's been fathered by a firm and loving father—there was friction, we all remember, with sadness and pain, but nevertheless there was plenty of love to go round. Jerome knows what it's like to *be* a teenage boy—it would be different if it were a girl—and don't forget he's had a head-start by having Luca as a pupil in his karate class. They'd work it out between them. Daniela's not naïve. If she and Jerome have chosen each other, she'd know what she was letting herself and her son in for. And she'll only do it if she really loves him.'

Craig was reluctantly silenced. As so often in conversation, his wife's persuasions overcame his hesitancy. She was more positive, more hopeful, and had more faith. He relied on his own abilities and believed the world was a harsh place where one had to outwit the opposing forces with knowledge, competency, and hard work. They lived by different stars.

May

Lord, I lift to you our Bible study group. Let there be no dissension among the Protestants and Catholics. A kind of cattiness seems to be intruding upon what has always been a harmonious atmosphere. And Grannie Mac keeps stirring the pot. Why does she always do this, Lord? What lies behind it? Give me wisdom, dear Lord, as I help lead this group. We want our times together to be pleasing to you, Lord, and to be beneficial to each person present, not detrimental or unsettling. May it be a truly ecumenical gathering. Help us to be channels of your grace.

It turned out that, like his mother, Daniela occasionally went on retreat. She had a weekend retreat coming up—apparently not very structured, more geared towards counselling—led by her parish priest. Jerome felt strangely familiar with the process—the anticipation, the hopes, the slight dread of the solitude involved, and the normally positive experience of feeling refreshed and renewed afterwards.

He offered to manage Luca's programme. Luca was due to spend the Friday night with a friend, and go to a Saturday morning movie. Jerome offered to pick the two friends up and take them to Spur for lunch, and wondered if Luca would like to spend Saturday night at his parents' place. His mother in particular would love having him over again. To her it was a joy having a teenager to care for again.

'Oh, Jerome, if you think your parents won't mind, I think Luca would love it. He really misses his grandparents, all four of them, and would enjoy being with friends their age. Just check with your mother first.'

'I will, but I can already assure you it'll be fine. Luca is the one we should be checking with.'

'We'll do that when the time comes.'

'And then he can go to church with my parents, and I'll join all of them for lunch. I'll give you a chance to settle back in at home before bringing Luca back. I know my mother always needs a bit of peace and quiet to adapt to being home again.'

'Oh, and I'll make supper for the three of us. I'd love to do that. Just something very simple.'

'If you want to, thanks, Daniela. We'll be happy consumers.'

And so it was all decided. Luca was intrigued by the plan, and pleased with it.

Daniela and Jerome snatched a coffee together before she set off, and Jerome had a strangely free evening. Daniela and her son had crept into his heart and seemingly every crevice of his life, so that strangely he almost felt at a loose end without them. He normally revelled in solitude but had grown unaccustomed to it in the past few months. He called his brother.

'What are you doing tonight, Matthew? Shall we go grab a pizza somewhere?'

'Good idea. Nicole has to rest, and I was just wondering what to do with myself. I'll meet you at Forries.'

'See you there, in about half an hour.'

The brothers had a beer or two, and a large pizza to share.

'How's it going with Nicole?' asked Jerome.

'Not too bad, thanks. Mercifully she's learnt to handle the pressure of the situation better than she did to start with. And the prognosis is still looking good, for which we are all grateful, as you can well imagine. How're things your side?'

'Good. I have to be careful not to get too distracted from my studies by the presence of Daniela and Luca in my life, but they are a real pleasure, not a pain. Luca sees in me a father figure, which is rather daunting, particularly as his view of a father is somewhat warped by his experience of Antonio. And Daniela verges on being clingy. Of course this takes some adjustment, as I've been a crusty old bachelor for years now. I'm not complaining, just gradually getting used to it.'

'Mum really likes both of them, and is very much hoping it'll all work out well for you.'

'Yes, I know that. I hope she won't be pushy though.'

'She seldom is.'

'Yes, you're right, she seldom is. We're pretty lucky.'

'Even with Nicole, she's been so supportive without overdoing it. And now she and Nicole's mother have become friends. I hope they don't become too chummy though—it might become a bit claustrophobic for me and Nicole, like feeling we're hemmed in by a maternal wall. But I think they're both sensible enough to restrict themselves to Bible study and Nicole's health, and to keep their hands off our relationship. We'd hate a running commentary.'

'Ya, I think you can rest assured they'll spare you that.'

In parting, Jerome asked Matthew, 'Do you think you'd like to join me and Luca for lunch at Spur tomorrow with one of his friends? You know, someone of my own age might be nice to help ward off the boisterous teenage energy they might be displaying after being cooped up for a couple of hours with their movie?'

'I'll talk to Nicole and let you know.'

'Okay. Thanks for joining me this evening. I was suddenly glad I had a brother, something I normally take for granted.'

Matthew affectionately punched Jerome on his upper arm and went back to his place feeling strengthened. We should see each other independently of Mum and Dad more often, he thought to himself.

He didn't join Jerome for lunch the next day but was still happy to have been invited.

Jerome's lunch with the teenagers was perfectly fine. He was treated to a blow by blow account of their movie, which took all strain out of conversation, and the next day's lunch was fine too.

Craig and Jerome were both focused on Luca, which meant neither of them was invested in generating any kind of friction between themselves. Clare heaved a sigh of relief and was simply focused on producing the best meal and atmosphere she possibly could. Having Luca was a treat.

Regrouping at Daniela's place felt slightly strange—she seemed quieter and more thoughtful than usual—but Jerome was semi-prepared for this, and concentrated on Luca making an easy transition from his busy weekend back to his home life.

He left early, to give Daniela and Luca space to reconnect as the loving mother and son they were. Grateful, Jerome pulled out his most difficult textbook and knuckled down to some serious studying.

In the meantime, Clare was once again experiencing the preoccupation of the Catholic Church with Mary, particularly during the month of May. Mary loomed large in the life of the Church. Clare knew that and was somewhat ambivalent about it. As a child she had of course been taught the rosary in catechism classes but it was not common practice to recite it in her childhood home. Now that she was part of an ecumenical Bible study group, she was well aware of her Evangelical friends' suspicion of and even hostility to the near-deification of Mary. Was Mary not simply the humble instrument, who died normally, and went the way of all believers, to be resurrected at the return of Christ?

Craig was adamant that the Catholic Church had more than embellished the truth and had its own motives—mixed, as always—for elevating Mary to being immaculately conceived and assumed into heaven. She was the Mother of Christ and as such deserved a special place but was surely not equal to God. To many Catholics she was in fact a goddess, much like the pagan goddesses of old, and perhaps a Catholic trade-off to appease the pagan influences operative in the early Church.

Whatever the 'truth', Clare was confused. She felt a certain animosity to the demand for an all-out devotion to the person of Mary, whom one was required to follow almost to the exclusion of all else, it appeared, but she knew that Catholics in general held together the worship of God, the presence of angels, the communion of saints and the veneration of Mary within an easier balance than she had ever been able to muster.

Clare was pensive. How could she gain clarity? Her relationship with Sister Bridget ran deep but there were some subjects it was nevertheless difficult to broach.

Perhaps they could talk about Mary's role in the Christian Church generally and her place in the life of the individual believer specifically. This would seem less personal and intrusive, surely, than asking Sister Bridget about her own beliefs, and in fact it was the proper level for Clare to make her own assessment. She wanted greater intimacy with the Mother of her Lord if it could be had without compromising her faith in himself as part of the Trinity. It was a quandary for her, and one she longed to have resolved. So she decided she needed to talk to Sister Bridget after all. Hopefully she would be frank. Clare would try to be indirect in her approach. When they were next together, they had hardly had a sip of tea when Clare broached the subject.

'Do you believe in the Assumption of the Blessed Mary into heaven?' Despite her best intentions, Clare nevertheless found herself putting Sister Bridget on the spot.

'I'm not sure that I need to,' she rather refreshingly replied. 'It was a dogma brought in to help restore people's faith in the dignity of the human being after Europe had been decimated by two World Wars. I don't engage with it on a literal level.'

This was a great start, Clare felt. What else could she ask?

'Does Mary ever vie for position with Christ?' she wanted to know. This was the crux of her reservations.

'Not at all,' Sister Bridget appeared to be unfazed by the directness and nature of Clare's questions. 'Mary as the Mother of Jesus always—and I mean always—points to him, and not to herself. She is the servant of her Lord, as his other disciples and apostles also are.'

'But what about the people who practically worship Mary?'

'That is wrong, and idolatry, no less.'

'What is the Church doing about it, though?'

'Well, in some churches the priests themselves are guilty of it. In others, they try to steer the congregation into a healthier way of thinking, but all the icons and statues and general adulation of Mary can be unhelpful in this regard. Clare, I sense this is troubling you.'

'Yes, it is. How do you suggest I best proceed?'

'Start with where you are at—never discard that position out of hand. Then ask the Lord himself to confirm in you that which is true and pleasing to him and to strengthen your faith where it is weak. Specifically, lift up the whole question of Mary's place in *your* life to him and ask him to lead and guide you into the proper relationship with her for *you*. He will do so, you'll see.'

'You really think that is the way, Sister Bridget? Is that not shelving my own responsibility to find out the truth?'

'It will nevertheless be *your* truth, and prayer is the best way to arrive at that.'

Suddenly the problem seemed to have assumed life-size proportions and not to be so overwhelming and grand. Clare could not be expected to resolve the complex question for the whole of the Catholic Church—not even the Pope could be expected to do that—so how could she, as an individual believer, take it on? It was folly, she suddenly realized. Sister Bridget was right. The Lord would help her resolve the issue in the context of her own faith. What a relief! She felt reassured and decided to let the matter rest, at least for the moment. It would find its own place in the context of her larger faith.

Clare soon decided that she would discuss these questions with Father Sean as well. When she next went to confession, she would ask him if she could discuss the topic of Mary with him. She knew his views were unorthodox, and maybe that was just what she needed to hear.

Father Sean listened to her questions but did not attempt to answer them directly. He simply hoped that his responses would help her feel her way through her quandary. Nevertheless, he was disarmingly honest.

Clare stated her belief in God as Holy Trinity. Father Sean agreed.

'Believing in Mary need not detract from our belief in God as Father, Son and Holy Spirit, but as the Mother of our Lord, as the first saint, as the first one to assent to his presence in her life, she surely deserves a special place in ours.'

This did make sense, Clare thought to herself. But she had some more unanswered questions, and this was her opportunity,

'But what about the Immaculate Conception and the Assumption into heaven, Father Sean? Surely this places her on the level of a deity?'

'Not at all, Clare, not at all. She was indeed fully human but it is surely unthinkable that someone as pure and saintly and—dare I say it?—sinless as Mary should be subject to the same original sin at the start of life and decay at the end of life as the rest of us?'

Not unthinkable at all, Clare said to herself. The contrary was in fact inconceivable. Mary was subject to mortality, surely, or she would not be fully human.

But she did not say this much as she did not want to debate the issue with Father Sean. She wanted to learn from him, and she realized he had been pondering these perplexities a lot longer and with a lot more learning than she had. So she would keep most of her reservations about what he was saying to herself.

Their conversation continued.

'However, Clare, there is a great deal of superstition around the person of Mary. She is viewed by many Catholics as a kind of talisman, someone who can be flattered, cajoled and manipulated into providing miracle cures and favours. I do not believe in her in this way at all.'

Father Sean was emphatic.

'I also do not see her as the kind of female side of God, as in an animus-anima type of duo, as some people do.'

Clare knew exactly what he was talking about, and was very relieved to hear him counter this belief so robustly.

'I see her instead as a great example to be followed—in her submission to our Lord, in her faith in him, in her faithfulness to him right up to the point of his death. Without a doubt she encouraged the other disciples, she was also the greatest of the apostles . . . She was the first person to know who Christ was, and to follow him.'

Here Clare felt Father Sean was getting carried away. How did he know these things? On what were they based? Like so many things in the Catholic Church, as Father Sean confirmed, they were based on 'tradition', on the dogma of the Catholic Church itself, rather than on Scripture, on which her Evangelical and Protestant friends based their faith.

She had not expected to have all her questions answered, all her puzzles resolved. But she knew that Father Sean's honesty was very reassuring. He too did not necessarily accept all the 'rumours' about apparitions of Mary that were bandied about though discounted none, but with great humility he expressed his own appreciation of her in terms which still eluded Clare. 'Our blessed Lady, our holy Mother' were terms which were not natural to Clare, even though she had been a Catholic all her life. She would say the rosary more often, she resolved. Calling on Mary as the Mother of God always challenged her faith, and she would continue to submit to the discipline of this age-old practice.

She left Father Sean simultaneously reassured and challenged. In comparison to their conversation about Mary, confession had been simple and, as usual, provided encouragement.

When she got home, she simply told Craig, 'I've been to see Father Sean today. He was helpful.'

She decided to have a quiet time with her journal, her Bible lying on the table beside it. She reflected for a while, and then went through to the kitchen to make lunch.

'I'd like us to invite Father Sean round for dinner one of these days, darling, maybe at the same time as your mother. As different as they are in their beliefs, I think it would nevertheless be a pleasant evening.'

'If you think my mother would enjoy it, sweetheart, that would be fine by me. You understand these group dynamics a lot better than I do. What I like about Father Sean is that we can enjoy a good whisky together and he also follows rugby. I enjoy him.'

'That settles that then,' she said, smiling, satisfied with her morning's work.

Besides her ongoing study of Julian of Norwich, Clare had just finished rereading *Middlemarch*. She wrote in her journal:

> *A novel is a work of the imagination. It draws the reader into its circle of society made up of characters, their lives, their motives, their interrelations, their interactions, their commitments, their development. The reader becomes part of the observing, judging, experiential flux of life as portrayed in the fictional work. The moral tone may or may not coincide with the reader's own position but, for the period of reading, disbelief is ideally suspended.*

At least this is what Clare believed. She needed a cup of tea to reorientate herself into her present chronology and space. Did she know any Bulstrodes, any Casaubons, any Rosamond Vincys? Possibly, in a less caricatured version—more complex, less recognizable . . . And, more to the point, did she have any of their despicable tendencies herself?

Sipping her tea, she tried to survey her most common motives for doing things, or refraining from doing them, and found this process to be perhaps even trickier than that of the novelist creating motives and character traits with her pen. After due self-examination, and a prayer for insight into herself, she tentatively concluded that she was usually generous and kind-hearted, and only hoped these traits were genuine and not the result of a desire to appear righteous in the eyes of her neighbours. *If that is the case, dear Lord, forgive me, and help me to be motivated purely by love of you.*

She proceeded to water her herb garden, put her grocery list in her handbag, and give Elsa some instructions for cleaning out the garage. She would stop by for a cup of tea with her mother-in-law on her way back. Clare thanked God for the uncomplicated happiness she experienced in her daily life. Craig was a major part of it, as were her sons, but she knew they were not the source. It flowed from her relationship with her Creator, and he had given them to one another to be a mutual source of blessing, of comfort and of growth.

Clare had learnt over the years that she needed to declare war on her natural human selfishness. It was so normal to consider one's own point of view before all else, and then dwell on the effects of others' actions on one's own situation, that it took disciplined effort and willpower to extend one's horizons to give equal consideration to the validity of the position of others.

Clare had discovered this over the many years of loving, caring and praying for those she loved and even for those she did not know. She had learnt to extend herself and to imagine herself in the skin of another. She had indeed grown into a compassionate person. While not openly acknowledged most of the time, this was in fact appreciated by almost all who knew her.

A few days later Clare found herself paging through an old journal. It emanated from her student days. She was sorting through a cupboard in a drive to freshen up her bedroom. It needed unburdening from the weight of the past.

It was the summer of 1979. She had just turned twenty-one, and her father had given her a trip to Israel, where she had longed to go ever since she was a child in catechism. She was to go with a friend of her choice. Naturally she chose Monica, her best friend from their schooldays, whose parents fortunately were game.

They set off on the 30th of November, soon after their exams. It was to be a three-week trip.

Arriving at Tel Aviv airport with its security checks and somewhat hostile atmosphere was an intimidating start but on exiting the inner area they were met by their guide, Meschach, an excitable but friendly Israeli, who was also a Christian, quite a rare combination, they were to discover.

They were taken to a youth hostel in Jerusalem, told which part of the city they were to explore that day, and to be ready to be picked up by Meschach at ten the next morning. Freedom! they thought, thanked him and settled in to the extent that it was possible. Giggling with excitement, they walked in the direction of the old city.

Once there, they were fascinated and almost overwhelmed. Clinging to each other, they tried to duck and dive in an attempt to shake off the vendors, mostly without success. They had their money belts tied securely around their waists, with one arm they were clutching each other, and with the other arm warding off the Arab vendors, desperate to exchange sentimental memorabilia for dollars. They knew that the very next day they would walk the Via Dolorosa to the Holy Sepulchre, today was just for orientation and personal exploration.

After resisting everything but an icon each, they finally wrenched themselves away from the magnetic hustle and bustle, and went to a nearby market which Meschach had indicated as a good place to stock up on fresh produce as needed. They were too protective of their travel allowance to go out to dinner and, weary as they were by this stage, after the trip and their sortie, they decided they'd make ratatouille at the hostel. They shopped accordingly.

The biggest and healthiest aubergines they'd ever seen, fresh tomatoes, onions, large baby marrows and more, they felt they were living a page out of a health magazine. Throwing everything together was fun and devouring a large plate each a pleasure. This was to be the first of many such meals. Ever after Clare associated ratatouille with this time in her life.

The next day proved quite gruelling. They had each in their different ways imagined that this pilgrimage would be like a three-dimensional Sunday school lesson. But it was quite the contrary.

Yesterday's Arabs were today's intruders and, far from meditating on Christ's passion as they walked, they spent another couple of hours warding off vendors. What Clare found most distressing was the way the Church of the Holy

Sepulchre was carved up into different denominations, each vying with the other for supremacy. The most gentle soul of all was the Ethiopian priest who explained some of the background and significance of the various facets of the Church to them. The gaudiness of the gold chandeliers right at the spot where Christ was supposed to have been crucified struck Clare as incongruous in the extreme. Why could there not simply be a wooden cross, or a crucifix? She realized she shared some of Monica's Protestant leanings towards simplicity and lack of ostentation.

In the weeks that followed they took trips to Bethlehem and the chapel where representations of Mary's exposed breasts as she suckled the infant Jesus almost swallowed them up. They went to Jericho, the Dead Sea, Masada, and stood in the very place from which Ezekiel had seen his vision of the dead bones coming to life.

They explored Haifa and Safed, spent a full day in Nazareth and, of course, closer to where they were living, walked the Mount of Olives and the hills of Capernaum, took a boat across the Sea of Galilee, and ate fish at St Peter's restaurant. Now the Biblical stories did indeed spring to life, and both of them felt that everything was much smaller and more familiar than their childhood imagination with its exaggerations and distortions had pictured. The Mount of Olives was not Table Mountain, and its goats and olive trees gave it a homely feel.

Christ was brought closer to them, and they did not forget to say their prayers, sometimes together, but most times individually, in what stillness their hearts could muster.

The day of departure drew near far too soon for their liking, but they knew they were enriched and would be able to unwrap some of their vivid experiences back home. They both embraced their parents, who all four met them at the airport and surprised them by taking them to lunch at the Mount Nelson. They were truly home, in good old South Africa, with its colonial baggage, its excessive privilege for the likes of them, and its welcome but now strange familiarity. Their travels, however, would mark their understanding of Biblical times and places in an indelible way.

Clare was still sitting on the floor, with the journal in her hands, when Craig walked in to fetch his pills.

'I forgot to take these this morning. What on earth are you doing?' he asked her.

'Reliving my trip to Israel. Let's go there together sometime, Craig. We could even fit it in directly after our trip to Istanbul . . . I could do with a spiritual shot in the arm.'

'You could get that right here, at home, Clare, as you do daily. But if you really want to go back, I would take you in a separate trip. Remember though that Israel now is even less safe and secure than it was then. I quite wonder at your dad—though I admire him—for letting you young girls go.'

'We were young women, darling. We'd both just turned twenty-one.'

'I know, I know. All the same, he was brave, and I'm glad my future wife returned safely. Let's talk about it again, sweetheart. Now I can see you are under the spell of the Holy Land.'

'I guess I am. Let me pack this journal safely back where it belongs, and let's go and take a walk together in the garden. The birds will bring me back to reality, and it is a reality I love and greatly appreciate.'

With his arm around her shoulders they went to the garden, and Clare had an eerie premonition that after all they would never go to Israel together.

Winter

We stood by a pond that winter day,
And the sun was white, as though chidden of God,
And a few leaves lay on the starving sod;
   —They had fallen from an ash, and were gray.
      (From 'Neutral Tones' by Thomas Hardy, 1840-1928)

June

Soon Matthew will be married. Who could have anticipated such a wonderful outcome when we were all going through such grief regarding Nicole's health? Thank you, Lord.

When their big day, the 6th of June, dawned, Nicole and Matthew were both radiant. Their wedding was quiet, transparent and peaceful, just like them. Though still somewhat frail, Nicole nevertheless looked beautiful and totally in love with her childhood sweetheart. Her lacy wedding dress was as delicate as she was. Her veil softened what was left of the evidence of her illness, and was made of a fabric which suited her translucent personality. Walking down the aisle on her proud father's arm, happy as he was to have his daughter beside him rather than forever gone from him, Nicole looked as though she would rather run into Matthew's arms immediately than linger on her father's.

Matthew was glowing with welcoming joy and pride in his darling's triumph in her battle against death and he vowed to cherish her and appreciate her presence with him every day of their life together.

The ceremony went off smoothly, though many in the congregation were in tears, particularly Clare and Nicole's mother, Pam, tears of joy and relief that this moment had come to set them all free from the agony they had so recently endured.

The reception was held at Nicole's parents' home, strange that it would be her home no longer. It had so recently been her abode both night and day.

In Nicole's father's speech he barely made reference to her illness except as a 'difficult period' they had all come through. Nicole was quietly radiant and Matthew glowing with pride.

'My darling has emerged from the trial of her life,' Matthew started his speech. 'We wouldn't like to revisit any part of it, except its positive ending. Now the joy of looking forward awaits us, and all the enchantments ahead. Don't be surprised if you don't see too much of us for the next little while. We need to regroup into this new phase of our lives. We shall surely emerge in due course, and we shall be in touch. But thank you for understanding that we do need time to orientate ourselves after all Nicole has been through and after taking the big step we have today.'

The rest of the wedding consisted of a luncheon of smoked salmon, cream cheese, and salad, and other more wintry foods, followed by crème brûlée and coffee, accompanied by dancing for those who felt like it. Matthew did lead Nicole in the first dance, but they did not participate much more than that. Despite the champagne, and dancing, all took place against the backdrop of Nicole's recent illness so the atmosphere was slightly subdued though joyful. No one wanted to strain the young bride, least of all Matthew, who after dancing very gently with her, led her to a comfortable seat, from which she could interact with the guests, as they came to congratulate the newly-weds. Matthew also found time to circulate among family and the few friends who were gathered there but every couple of minutes he would be at his darling's side, to reassure her and to make certain she wasn't taking too much strain.

Clare watched in wonder. This was her beloved son, who it seemed so recently was proudly showing off the drawings he'd done at primary school. Now he was showing off his bride.

Once Matthew felt Nicole had had enough excitement for one day, he quietly took leave of both sets of parents and simply vanished from the scene, leaving the guests to continue enjoying the gathering. Their cottage was ready. There would be time enough for a honeymoon at a later stage.

Matthew and Nicole were now one.

Clare was exhausted but fulfilled at the end of it all. Craig seemed more exhausted still, without them really knowing why. So, unusually for them, they both lay down together, mulling over the ceremony and reception.

'They both looked very happy, and that's the main thing,' observed Clare.

'Yes, they did, sweetheart, and so did you. You looked totally beautiful—just as you always do.'

'Thank you, darling. How kind of you to say so, and to think so!'

Craig soon fell into a deep sleep, while Clare read a while and then got up to make some tea.

By the time Craig emerged it was getting dark.

'Let's have some soup for supper, darling. Would that be fine?'

'Comforting, and delicious, sweetheart. What kind are we having today?'

'Pea-soup and ham, with croutons.'

'Superb. I'll spend a few minutes in my study while you get it ready.'

On his son's wedding day . . . Even Clare was somewhat surprised, but not very. She knew her husband's drive and determination. She had long since accepted his will to succeed as an integral part of his persona and, although it occasionally left her lonely, she was grateful for the enjoyment he clearly derived from his work.

They had a peaceful supper and, as usual, Clare retired for the night some time before Craig, both of them very content with their day's work. Matthew and Nicole had found their life's partner in each other. Jerome would soon follow suit. There was enough to be grateful for in one day.

July

Istanbul is looming, Lord, and I am both apprehensive and excited. Keep me steady. May the blend of cultures and fusion of continents not confuse or destabilise me, Lord. Help me to keep my balance and be a blessing and good companion to Craig as he attends this conference which is so important to him.

A s much as she'd wanted to go to Istanbul, so ill at ease did Clare feel once she got there. The chaotic behaviour of the taxis in the out-of-control traffic, the pollution manifesting in the stenches emanating from various points along the streets, the thronging crowds, the stifling humidity, the invasive leering of lecherous men all conspired to make her long for the sanctuary of the life she had left behind her. Clare felt culturally disembodied. She had no sense of belonging in this strange place where they spoke a foreign tongue and behaved in foreign ways. Foreign only to her, of course, but that made her feel all the more alienated. Craig was not being very helpful. Impatient with her anxiety and her nerves and spouting the occasional lecture admonishing her to get a hold of herself, he only added to her sense of being ill at ease, of not being at home. And the more he painted pictures of where and how they could live in

Turkey, using it as a base for exploring the eight neighbouring countries, the more jittery she felt.

Before too long Clare and Craig had a blazing row. It was triggered by her stress when using taxis. Craig accused Clare of being unnecessarily anxious—and she *was* anxious—to be safe, to get back to her sons, to be part of their future with their loved ones.

After a day or two, Clare gradually came to herself. She moved beyond her anxiety and into the world around her, where people were walking, arguing, loving, smiling, tired, happy or sad. In sheer self-defence she turned her back on her panic and willed herself into identifying with her moment-by-moment experience in the present time and space. Suddenly Craig's arm around her waist became reassuring rather than a useless barrier between herself and certain death.

Istanbul certainly had its glories. The Bosphorus was unsurpassable. On a ferry and by foot Clare and Craig explored its wonders big and small. With the waters lapping their feet they ate local dishes and talked more freely than usual. Clare made a concerted effort not to make Jerome or Matthew the centre of their conversation.

On their last evening, they went to an upmarket Indian restaurant boasting international cuisine. After placing their order, Clare and Craig took a stroll down memory lane reminiscing about their first meeting twenty-nine years ago. It was the kind of stroll that basked in the present and looked to the future.

'I was preparing some material for the School Board meeting in the secretary's office. I looked up and there you were, this goddess in a royal blue frock, radiant with love and joy. You were so young, so beautiful, so innocent, how was I going to make you mine?'

'And then my pupils' Art Exhibition came up, and because we'd invited Board members, you were there too. Suddenly we were talking. You particularly liked the depiction of Titania and Bottom one of my students had painted, and so we got talking about Shakespeare and *A Midsummer Night's Dream*. You invited me to *The Tempest*, which was showing at Maynardville. It turned out you knew extracts by heart . . .'

'And I still do:

> *. . . the isle is full of noises,*
> *Sounds and sweet airs, that give delight, and hurt not.*
> *Sometimes a thousand twangling instruments*
> *Will hum about mine ears; and sometime voices,*
> *That, if I then had wak'd after long sleep,*
> *Will make me sleep again: and then, in dreaming,*
> *The clouds methought would open, and show riches*
> *Ready to drop upon me; that, when I wak'd,*
> *I cried to dream again.*

And after that night we shared our own dream and never looked back again, did we, my sweetheart?'

'No, we didn't, unless we count tonight as a happy way of looking back.'

'I remember sitting next to you at Maynardville, not sure whether I could take your hand, which lay in your lap so invitingly . . . But the tones of your voice, and your general demeanour, were so gentle, so encouraging, that I took the chance, very nervous in case I was making the wrong move and would put you off.'

'Yes, I remember how sweet you were, darling, how tentative. But over coffee afterwards we could talk a bit more, and agree to "date cautiously"—I think that was the sweet, old-fashioned term you used, and quite typical I may now say it was, but at the time I found it simply charming, and it made me feel surprisingly safe. And we scheduled our next date—it was to be dinner at Kelvin Grove, remember?'

'I do. And once again you looked ravishing. I had to pinch myself to believe that such a beautiful princess was gracing my arm, adorning my table, and I had to remind myself that you were a sensitive, intelligent young woman, and not simply a beautiful doll on which I could feast my eyes.'

'Oh, yes, we talked—about many things, so you definitely got to know how I thought and what I felt about politics, faith, art, culture . . . Talking about families took us several months more but it was then that I knew I wanted our bond to be lasting.'

'I think I knew that well before you did, sweetheart. I was smitten pretty much right from the start, whereas you grew into a realization of our suitability far more gradually. I'm so glad the verdict when it finally did come was positive. I would have been crushed if I'd lost you.'

'I think the Lord's hand was guiding us right from the start, darling, putting just the right conductors in our way for us to grow together. Do you remember when you asked me to marry you?'

'Of course I do. We were at the sea. I had my arms around your waist, we were sitting on a rock, looking at the waves breaking all around us, and I was whispering gently in your ear, hoping it would melt any resistance there might be in your heart.'

'Oh, but there was none, I longed to melt into you and be yours forever. I had been feeling that for several weeks by then, and I was eager to move to the next level . . . and then the magical words came: "Will you marry me, dearest Clare?" The way you asked was so sweet, and so full of love, that alone would have melted any resistance if there had been any. Instead, you had a willing slave! Here I still am, devoted to you, my darling, beyond imagination. Not even I—so in love then—could have foreseen the depths our love would reach. Having children together and loving our sons has surely taken us both into a dimension we never knew was there. And they are such wonderful young men now . . .'

Oops, Clare was happy the dessert menu had arrived. It would help her rediscover her balance in this romantic interchange. She knew that she so often brought the conversation to rest on Jerome and Matthew, and she was forever trying to train herself not to do that, to allow Craig to be the sole centre of her focus. But then it was natural, was it not, that their love which culminated in the lives of these two young men would linger on reflecting on them too? But she knew it jarred with Craig when he felt he was but a route to motherhood, and overlooked as her husband in his own right.

The waitress was charming, dressed in traditional Indian garb, and the moment of tension for Clare passed. She knew she shouldn't be so self-conscious with Craig, especially when extolling the merits of his very own sons, but experience had taught her this was an area where she needed to tread very lightly.

Eventually it was time to take another gentle stroll, this time through the streets of the old city on the way back to their quaint hotel.

During the days that Craig attended his conference, Clare was able to relax occasionally and explored the area of Bebeck right on the Bosphorus on her own. Here she felt relatively safe. There were people everywhere enjoying the surroundings just as she was. When she saw a single man approaching, she simply crossed the street and merged with the inevitable throng of people there. Paranoid? Perhaps. But she had been warned to be wary of strange men who tried to engage her in conversation and then forcibly demanded more.

On the evening of the conference gala dinner she dressed up in the black silk dress and diamond jewellery she tended to wear on such occasions. The economists who were assembled there were good, sound people rather than scintillating conversationalists. Nevertheless, Clare enjoyed herself. It was particularly gratifying to see Craig among his peers. He came alive in a way she hadn't seen for a long time, and she felt a pang of guilt for perhaps not creating the milieu for him to express himself more freely. Her own preoccupations were more than likely the ones which dominated the household, and Craig was accommodating to a fault. How could she ever doubt him?

It was true that she didn't doubt his love but she did occasionally doubt his capacity to embrace her and their sons with compassion and understanding. He seemed less than sensitive to their needs at times and rather heavy-handed in his approach. But Craig was who he was and she could not change him. Pleading for sympathy tended to make things worse rather than better, and under no circumstances did she want to risk that. Clare's mother had displayed manic-depressive tendencies, which had disturbed the rhythm of their family and caused her children much suffering. Clare came to value serenity and balance very highly as a result. This was all the more reason that feeling so unsettled in Istanbul was experienced as deeply threatening, and with Craig, her protector, turning against her at times, she felt acutely vulnerable and looked forward to returning to the haven that was her home.

Their last day was refreshingly pleasant. They went back to the Grand Bazaar to get some gifts for Daniela and Nicole, and Sister Bridget and Pam. The beautiful cloths and silks caught the imagination and made one grateful there were loved ones to take things home to. She loaded up on Turkish delight for her sons, a childhood treat that had lasted into adulthood as a favourite. Clare also bought a beautiful cloth for the large coffee table in her lounge.

After dropping off their shopping at their hotel, Clare and Craig proceeded to mosey into alleys and byways as yet undiscovered by them. Not only did they find quaint shops with Persian carpets and exquisite ceramics, pottery and sculptures but also attractive residential areas. Clare could read Craig's mind—he was seriously indulging in the possibility of their acquiring an apartment in Istanbul. He tried to sell her the idea but indirectly, not wanting to stir dissent. Clare tried to empathise with his muted enthusiasm but didn't want to raise his hopes. She knew she could never live in Turkey, not even for a few months a year. Two weeks of her life were a sufficient investment. *Forgive me for being so blinkered, Lord. I depend on you to change my mind if it needs to change.* Clare suspected she was being cowardly but decided to leave the matter in the hands of her Lord and trust her husband to understand her and have compassion on her weakness.

August

It is blissful to be home, Lord. How I feared I might not make it. Forgive me for my unbelief. Bless us, Lord—Craig and me, Jerome, Daniela and Luca, Matthew and Nicole, her family, Grannie Mac—all our loved ones, precious Lord. And help us to be a blessing in the world.

One of the pleasures of being back home was to be surrounded by her favourite books. Henry Tilney from *Northanger Abbey* was Clare's favourite Jane Austen hero, and Elizabeth Bennett from *Pride and Prejudice* her favourite heroine. She further appreciated Jane Austen's eulogy to the novel in *Northanger Abbey* and had it typed up and stuck on her fridge, so that Craig would remember not to be dismissive of her reading material. He tended to think English literature began with Shakespeare and ended with Dickens, and Clare believed he secretly pooh-poohed women writers in general. Clare would have none of it. Jane Austen, the Brontë sisters, George Eliot, and more modern novelists such as Virginia Woolf and Arundhati Roy, all demanded the highest respect. Craig had to recognize this—it was important to her.

And so Craig daily had to pass the page on the fridge which exhorted novelists to promote the reading of novels by their heroines, almost as though he were being accused of being such a thoughtless novelist himself:

Alas! if the heroine of one novel be not patronized by the heroine of another, from whom can she expect protection and regard? I cannot approve of it . . . Let us not desert one another; we are an injured body . . . There seems almost a general wish of decrying the capacity and undervaluing the labour of the novelist, and of slighting the performances which have only genius, wit, and taste to recommend them . . .—'And what are you reading, Miss?'—'Oh, it is only a novel?' replies the young lady, while she lays down her book with affected indifference, or momentary shame . . . It is, in short, only some work in which the greatest powers of the mind are displayed, in which the most thorough knowledge of human nature, the happiest delineation of its varieties, the liveliest effusions of wit and humour are conveyed to the world in the best chosen language.

Clare felt this was definitive. And so did beleaguered Craig, after sufficiently long and daily exposure to Jane Austen and his wife's point of view.

There was in fact more intellectual companionship between the two than might at first appear, and their emotional bonding was naturally deep. But, despite the unpredictable role reversal that occurred in Turkey, Clare was generally the creative one, always wanting to explore new frontiers of thinking, feeling and representing, while Craig looked at what already existed in the world of facts and economics. Craig was occupied with warding off the potential dangers of the future, while Clare usually embraced the future as the opportunity to try out new things. Deep down, however, she knew that the entire basis of her existence depended on the provision and support of her husband.

And of course there was mutual respect between them—a lot. Craig never belittled Clare's artistic endeavours and she never showed him that she found much of his work dull. This would have been disrespectful though she suspected he had a fair idea that economics was not a riveting world to her. She was enormously grateful to him for providing stability for her and their sons to develop their own lives freely and safely, without anxiety about bread-and-butter issues. She knew Jerome and Matthew took this somewhat for granted—even though she had tried to instil a sense of gratitude in them. They knew nothing else—unlike her, whose father had at one stage been made redundant at the school where he was headmaster. It had been a devastating blow to her mother, her brother Duncan and herself. She tried to help Jerome and Matthew appreciate how fortunate they were not to have had to deal with anything of that nature, and this was largely due to Craig's hard work, competence and foresight. She also regularly expressed her gratitude to her husband, and he appreciated this.

'You are welcome, sweetheart,' he would say, squeezing her hand. 'It is the least I can do for you. It is one way I have of showing you and the boys that I love you. And I hope they will in turn do the same for their families one day.'

'I am sure they will, darling. You have been such a shining example to them. I would hope and pray that they will follow closely in your footsteps.'

'And, in turn, I hope they have been wise enough to choose a wife who resembles you as closely as possible. You are my deepest blessing, sweetheart, and I pray that they have each found a woman who can be that for them.'

'Well, darling, with regard to Nicole, our prayers for a full recovery for her have been answered. She and Matthew are so devoted to each other that I am sure they will be the deepest blessing to each other. Jerome is more complex—he needs to be understood by the woman he marries.'

'I have my doubts about Daniela if it is to be her. Let me say no more than that.'

Despite his initial reservations, there were many issues on which Craig had come round to Clare's way of thinking. Clare never ceased to appreciate that he was in fact more flexible than he at first appeared, and she never ceased to give thanks for him. *Bless him, Lord, and thank you for his presence in my life, and that he is so loving and dependable. May I in turn continue to be a blessing to him. Thank you, dearest Lord.*

The time came to go to sleep. Clare snuggled up to him, closed her eyes and was gone.

When she woke up the next morning, it was with a sense of joyful anticipation. Unlike her friends, Clare was not a great maker of 'To do' lists but she did believe in writing down some of her goals and aspirations. This was one way of holding herself accountable, she felt. Occasionally, no, quite frequently, she shared some of these concerns with Craig, or with a praying friend.

One of her prayers had been to 'let go' of Jerome. Writing this down seemed peculiar, and yet it was an indication of how important it was to her. It was of course difficult to 'achieve' in concrete terms, but having it written down in her journal kept her aware of the direction of travel in which she needed to go.

How was she faring?

Clare knew that too much introspection was self-defeating as it made one inward- rather than outward-bound. But in a case like this she did not want to deceive herself.

She looked at her reaction to Jerome's choice of Daniela. *I did not overreact, Lord, to her being a divorcée with a teenage son, older than him, and Italian . . . I could have.* She felt reassured, and she knew she was right to respond as she had—supportively, with acceptance, even being there as a loving adult for Luca. *How do I keep supporting all three of them,*

Lord, and yet be certain not to interfere? She felt encouraged to continue on the path she was on. *Thank you, Lord, thank you for your guidance. And help me not to be self-righteous, or smug.*

And Clare felt lighter, more peaceful, less anxious.

It was barely an hour after one of these prayers that Jerome called her and invited her to meet him and Daniela at the Vineyard Hotel for a drink, if possible with Craig. Clare suspected their announcement but didn't want to make premature assumptions.

'Try not to express disapproval, darling, whatever they might share with us,' she pleaded with Craig.

'Hi, Mum. Hi, Dad.'

'Hello, Daniela. Hello, Jerome,' they both said.

'Tell us about your trip, Mum.' Jerome and Daniela received their gifts with restrained pleasure. The atmosphere was tense. Something clearly was afoot.

After hearing some humorous and colourful sketches of their time in Istanbul, Jerome cut straight to the chase.

'Daniela and I are planning to get married. We would like your blessing.'

'That's wonderful, darling. Congratulations.' Clare took Daniela by both hands and kissed her lightly on each cheek. She gave Jerome a hug. 'We hope that you will be very happy together. Oh, and Luca will be part of the family! It seems he already is. What a delight this is to us.' She was so proud of Jerome, this strong man taking it upon himself to love, care for and nurture this beautiful, vulnerable woman and her son. In fact, he was already doing it but now he was making a commitment to carry her through life's trials. Equally, he was opening himself to receiving her love and having her at his side though the vicissitudes of life. Her heart swelled with emotion.

Craig was stiff, trying not to appear sullen, but clearly less than delighted. Sometimes he wished Clare would speak for herself alone and not say 'we' when she in no way represented his feelings. He managed to be civil, but only just.

Clare felt for Daniela. She was a sensitive person and would without a doubt be hurt by Craig's attitude, but it could not be helped. She had no control over his behaviour. She had tried to exercise her influence and been less than successful. Oh, surely he would come round in time.

On the way home Clare and Craig were both quiet, locked in their different thoughts and responses. Clare tried hard not to reproach Craig but she knew her silence would probably be construed as reproachful. *So be it, Lord*, she prayed. *I'm disappointed in him.*

A few days later Jerome approached her for a loan to put down a deposit on a house for them to live in once they were married. She understood why he spoke to her and not to Craig but this nevertheless placed her in an invidious position.

'Dad would obviously need to be in on this, darling, and I believe it will be better coming from you than from me in this instance. He holds the purse strings as you know, and this is your loan you are seeking, not mine.'

'I know, Mum, but I find him so unapproachable. He is sometimes falsely hearty and then, when it comes down to brass tacks, he becomes formal, distant and aloof. Can't you at least broach the subject with him? Afterwards I can have a formal consultation with him in his study, as though I were one of his clients—as indeed I almost will be, as I intend to pay him interest. It's just that I don't have much of a credit record as I've tended to pay cash for things—which should in fact be rewarded but for which one is punished instead.'

Jerome spoke with some bitterness and Clare knew this was not his only grievance. Affirmative action was also a sharp disadvantage to him and many of his peers, who felt they were bearing the brunt of the sins of their forefathers.

'I'll think about it, Jerome, give me a day or two, and I'll let you know whether I've managed to open the way for you, or whether I expect you to do that for yourself. I'll do my best, darling. I'd like it to work out for you but I don't want to set out to help you and then the situation boomerangs on you instead. So just hold your horses for a day or two . . .'

'The only thing is, Mum, we could lose the house, as the sellers need proof of the capacity to put down a deposit.'

'Be patient, Jerome, I'll do my best.'

When Jerome had left, Clare made herself a fresh pot of tea and sat down in her favourite armchair in the lounge. *Help me, Lord, give me wisdom. Show me the way. And bless Jerome, Daniela and Luca, and if this house is right for them, please hold it. Protect their path. We all, including Craig, want what is best for them, dear Lord.*

Immediately Clare felt her spirits lift, and soon afterwards Craig walked into the lounge.

'I thought I heard an early pot of tea on the go, sweetheart, and thought I'd join you for a quick cup before I continue on a particularly difficult case.'

'I may have another one for you, darling.'

'Oh, really? That's unusual. What is it?'

'It's Jerome, darling. He's hoping we can help him with a loan for a deposit on a house for them. Because he's always paid cash for things, he doesn't have much of a credit rating.'

'I warned him about this a few years back,' Craig said in an irritated tone of voice. 'Why is that boy always so stubborn?'

Clare was silent, hurt at the rancour there still seemed to be between them. *Soften his heart, Lord,* she prayed.

They finished their tea in silence.

'I'll think about it,' Craig muttered as he returned to his office.

Clare made a particularly nice lunch, hoping to smooth ruffled feathers. Perhaps she could have been more diplomatic, prepared the way for Jerome's request more gently, but it was too late now. All she could do was create as harmonious an atmosphere as possible without recriminating herself or Craig. *Can we at least discuss it calmly, Lord?*

Craig appeared calm at lunch.

'We can help him, sweetheart. I'll charge him interest, just as he would pay at a bank, but I'll help him. He has proven himself to be responsible. He must make an appointment to see me, though, as any client would.'

'He'll do that, darling, but please,' she couldn't help pleading, 'don't forget he is our son.'

'I won't, of course, I won't, but Jerome has always needed a tough hand.'

'Not too tough, please, darling, don't humiliate him.'

'I'll be careful not to, Clare. Don't worry.'

The interview between father and son later on the same day seemed to go well, because Jerome was smiling afterwards.

'Thanks, Mum,' he whispered on his way out. 'I know you must have smoothed the way. The lion was gentle. You're a star!'

The deal went through without a hitch, and Jerome, Daniela and Luca had themselves a delightful cottage in Kenilworth, not too far from their work in Wynberg and fractionally closer to UCT Medical School for Jerome's studies than his previous apartment in Plumstead. They showed off their new home to Clare and Craig with pride. After a few renovations including a fresh coat of paint all round, they could promptly move in.

Clare was thrilled for them.

A few days later she got another call from Jerome. 'Hi, Mum, are you home?'

'Why, yes, darling. Do you want to pop round?'

'Yes, I'll be there in ten minutes or so. Daniela may be with me. Is Dad there?'

Gosh, what could it be now? Clare wondered to herself.

'Well, he is, but he's in a consultation with your old school-friend, Martin, right now.'

'Oh, that's no problem. We'll have a drink with you while the two of them finish up.'

Within no time, Jerome and Daniela were in the kitchen.

'Mum, I'm going to tell you first. I know you'll be happy.'

'What is it, darling?'

'Because the deal for the house went through so easily, we have decided on approximately a month from today that Daniela and I will be getting married.'

'Oh, Jerome, that's wonderful news.' She embraced Daniela, kissing her on both cheeks, then hugged Jerome with all her might.

'Oh, hello, Dad, hi, Martin,' Jerome shook hands with both of them. He had always slightly envied the easy relationship Martin had with Craig but he no longer cared so much about these things. He had a new focus. He was a grown man himself now, no longer a boy, craving the affection his father seemed incapable of giving him.

'Hello, Daniela,' Craig said, patting her hand. Jerome introduced her to Martin. Martin was looking well and also relieved. He had just been bringing Craig up to speed with the happy resolution of his personal affairs while they wrapped up some adjustments to his offshore investments.

'Dad, Martin, Daniela and I are getting married sooner rather than later. Not quite sure of the exact date yet, but very soon. We'll make sure we invite you to the simple ceremony, and that includes you, Martin. I already told Daniela I'd like you to be our chief witness. It's great having a buddy who's a lawyer!'

'Sure, Jerome, and congratulations. I hope Daniela knows what she's in for!'

The bantering between the friends gave Craig a moment to catch his breath. His eyes turned to Clare and she nodded encouragingly. He had his reservations but decided to trust in the instincts of his wife, always closer to Jerome than he was, always more in sympathy with their elder son's needs and wants than he was. He knew Clare had been desperately disappointed over the years at the lack of understanding between father and son, and he made a concerted effort at this point not to add any further grief to the accumulation of wounds over the years.

'Congratulations again, son.' It was particularly touching to be addressed thus at this moment. Craig had always called Martin 'son', something which had riled Jerome over the years but which in this moment, in this positive moment of love and goodwill, he was ready to let go.

Having embraced Daniela—slightly awkwardly—Craig adopted a jovial tone. 'I think we have a bottle of champagne in the fridge, Clare, don't we? Now would be an excellent time for a toast.'

Toasts all round, though not without the usual slight tension between Jerome and his father, and there were more smiles and congratulations.

'The only one missing here is Luca,' Clare said.

'Oh, Clare, he has a huge project that needs to be handed in tomorrow, so we decided to leave him working with his project partner. But he'll be visiting soon enough. He loves coming here.'

'Please give him our best wishes, and our congratulations as well. He must be a happy boy!'

'He is. He's overjoyed.'

'Yes, Mum, he's over the moon. He wants to call me "Dad"—I'm still considering that one, because I would have had to be fourteen when I fathered him!—but he seems to think it would be the coolest thing.'

'And I agree with him, darling. Because that will be your role in his life. You have in effect been fathering him already. But of course that's for you three to work out.'

'Thanks, Mum, it's good getting your insights. We all three know you have a soft spot for Luca. He thrives on it.'

It was time for Martin to leave. Jerome saw him out.

'I'll get back to you with dates, buddy. We'll make sure we don't select a date on which you have an important court case.'

After a few more minutes of pleasantries with his parents, Jerome and Daniela left to go and have supper with Luca. Craig and Clare were left to themselves and their wonder.

'I'm very proud of Jerome, Craig. It is a brave choice.'

'I hope he doesn't live to regret it,' Craig responded.

'Let's pray that he won't, and be positive.'

'I'll do my best,' said Craig. 'That boy has always had a mind of his own, and has never asked for or taken my advice.'

'He's a grown man now, darling. Let's wish them all well. His decision shows courage. He's not afraid to take on far more responsibility than most men his age. I truly am proud of him. I wish you were too.'

'I have my reservations, Clare, but henceforth I'll keep them to myself.'

'Thank you, darling. If something is pressing, do share it. But I prefer to live with a thoroughly positive attitude to this new and vulnerable family still in its formation phase, and any negative energy surrounding their decision will therefore jar with me. So thank you for containing your reservations. Also, particularly when Luca is here, I'd like us to behave as we have always done—to treat him with warmth and affection, to affirm him.'

'Oh, no problem with Luca. He's a great kid.'

'Glad we can agree on that then. Let's eat.'

They ate in silence mostly, both working through their own emotions. It wasn't often that Clare discouraged Craig from speaking about his feelings to her—normally she was doing exactly the opposite—but in this case she truly didn't want a very special moment in the life of their son to be spoilt by a negative attitude on the part of his father. It had happened regularly in the past, and this would simply be once too often.

Clare went to bed early, to be alone with her thoughts, her prayers, her Lord. She loved her husband, but in this moment the needs of her son, Daniela and Luca seemed more pressing than Craig's. By the time he came to bed she had made peace with everything, including his reaction.

They kissed goodnight and she slept peacefully.

The next morning she wrote in her diary, *It is Duncan's birthday tomorrow. My parcel should have arrived by now and I know Sheila will give it to him on the day as a nice surprise. He has been wanting us to join them for Christmas for so long. Perhaps this year would be a good one to do so. I shall lean on you to guide us, Lord, you who are a loving Shepherd. Help us to hearken to your voice.*

Craig was to go on a business trip to the States towards the end of the year. It was decided that Clare would spend most of the time at her brother's place in Vermont as they both felt that would be more restful for her and also give her the opportunity to reconnect with her brother Duncan and his wife Sheila, and to get to know her nephew and niece a bit better. She was concerned about the strain all the travelling would be on Craig, but he was determined to do it.

'I need to establish some new links in order for my clients' investments to be expanded. Despite the crisis, after the UK, America is still the foremost country to do real business with as far as I'm concerned. We can fly via London on our way home.'

'I won't try and dissuade you from your strenuous programme, Craig, because I know I won't succeed. All I ask is that you make sure you get as much rest as possible, and remember to take your daily medication.'

'Don't worry about me, Clare, and don't try to mother me, sweetheart. You had your turn with Jerome and Matthew.' This was not the first time Craig had accused Clare of trying to mother him, and she found it particularly hurtful when her quite natural wifely concern was turned against her. 'You will be staying with Duncan and Sheila in order to relax, remember? If you spend your energy being anxious about me, it defeats the object.'

'Sorry, darling, I know I need to trust your good sense. I am just concerned, that's all, and it is because I love you.'

'I know, sweetheart, I know. All the same, it strains me to think of you worrying about me, so if you're relaxed, I'm able to concentrate on the objectives of my trip, instead of worrying about you worrying about me! Is that clear?'

Clare laughed. 'It is. I'll do my best.' *Remind me to pray, dear Lord, and give my burdens to you to bear. Help me never to put Craig in your place, especially when my anxiety is about him.* She felt chastised by her husband, and knew he probably had the right to feel frustrated. She also felt ever so slightly hurt. But she had to respect his need not to be mothered by her but trusted to be responsible and adult instead. In any case, this trip was still a few months away. There would be enough time to iron out the details. In the meantime, she would focus on living in the present and being as content and happy as possible among her family and friends, striving to be a blessing. *Above all, Lord, help me not to be a burden on Craig.* This was a refrain in her prayers, one she knew God was familiar with, but unlike her husband, she knew he never grew weary of hearing her concerns. His patience was infinite, his mercy never-ending. She resolved—as she so often did—to live even closer to him than before.

It was the tenth of August. Clare opened her Bible to Psalm 23. She was sitting at the kitchen table with a kola tonic and lemonade beside her. She reread it—not because she didn't know it by heart but because it was reassuring to see the words before her very eyes as well. She prayed this psalm over her children, and over their loved ones as well. Deeply comforted, as believers over the centuries have been, she chose to rest assured that the promises contained within it would come to pass.

Clare had supper on the go. Sometimes Craig kept her company in the kitchen, a glass of wine in his hand. At other times he sat in the lounge and caught up with some international—or local—news while she finished her preparations. Then there were times, like tonight, when he was so engrossed in his work that she had to go and call him. It was seven o' clock and Craig was not yet at the dinner-table. Was he trapped in an unusually long telephone conversation? She was happy that he had absorbing work to do. She knew that in a man's life—well, certainly in Craig's—work added a whole dimension of meaning.

If only he and his clients weren't at the mercy of the financial markets, but that was the nature of the beast. Craig was thoroughly conscientious and wanted to do the very best by each of his clients as well as by his fellow consultants, providing advice based on the latest information and most penetrating analysis.

Clare waited a few more minutes and then set off for his study. She walked down the passage deep in thought.

As she entered, her voice preceded her. 'Darling, it's . . .'

She stopped dead in her tracks. He was slumped over his desk. She rushed to his side, put her hand on his shoulder.

'Craig, sweetheart, talk to me, are you alright?' She shook him gently,

He didn't seem to be breathing.

'Craig, please, breathe, please . . .' She shook him more vigorously. No response.

'Oh, my God, what do I do?' she uttered out loud. 'Help me, Lord, help me, help me. This can't be true.'

She reached for the phone and dialled their house doctor's emergency number.

'Randall, this is Clare. Craig's not breathing. Come over immediately, please. Hurry! I don't know what to do.'

'I'm on my way, Clare. Try to keep calm.'

She shook him again, desperate. 'Breathe, Craig, breathe. Please. Wake up, darling. Don't leave me.'

Her heart was pounding. She could scarcely breathe herself.

As the headlights approached, she opened the gates. Randall Jennings was in Craig's study in no time.

'He's gone, Clare, he's gone. No pulse, no heart rate. He's been gone for about two hours already. There's nothing you could have done.'

Disbelief set in as Clare wrestled with herself and with what seemed to be Craig's unfathomable decision to depart from her so abruptly. She felt upset beyond endurance and yet simultaneously strangely numb.

'This can't be true, Randall. There was nothing wrong with him. What has caused this?'

'He did have an underlying heart condition, remember, Clare? One that was carefully controlled so none of us discussed it much. But with the additional burden of these volatile economic times weighing on him and on his clients, that is all one needs for the heart to give way under the pressure.'

Clare sat down, expressionless, and weak.

'I'm sorry, Clare, I'm so sorry.' He put his hand on her shoulder. 'There's nothing you, I, nor Craig himself could have done to prevent this. Our bodies, our organs are finite. Let's go through to the kitchen and get you a drink. It will help you catch your breath.'

He ushered her to the kitchen, poured her a whisky, and instructed her to call both her sons and summon them home immediately. She obeyed.

Jerome reached home first.

'What's wrong?' he barked. He looked pale and frightened.

'It's the worst news I could give you, Jerome. Dad has died, Jerome, Dad has died . . .'

Jerome's pallor intensified. 'What happened?' he wanted to know.

'A heart attack,' Randall Jennings replied. 'You know he had a heart condition and this was in all likelihood the result of an accumulation of stress. It was simply too much for his heart to cope with.'

Great sobs heaved through Clare. Dr Jennings allowed Jerome to comfort her. He tried to give them some privacy by going outside to wait for Matthew.

'Oh, Jerome, why didn't we pay more attention? Maybe we could have prevented it . . .'

'Mum, maybe we could have but most probably we couldn't. In any case, he's gone now.' Jerome sounded almost blunt.

'What shall I do, darling? How shall I live without him?'

'You'll depend more heavily on us, Mum, that's what you'll do.'

At which point Matthew walked in at the door.

He had already interacted with Dr Jennings and had his suspicions. When his fears were confirmed, he crumpled into a ball of grief and Jerome had to be strong for both his mother and now his brother.

'Matthew, you need to pull yourself together and be strong for Mum at this time.' Jerome spoke with some impatience.

'Let him be, Jerome, let him be,' Clare said, knowing that Matthew's sense of loss must be deeper than Jerome's. Clare noticed how she was beginning to think of things in the past tense. Does it happen so fast? she asked herself. Time itself seemed to have stood still altogether.

Jerome was in turmoil, for his mother, for his brother (whose softness often evoked impatience in him), and for himself—for the finality of the realization that he would never have the father he had spent his childhood longing for. Whatever chances he and Craig had had were gone forever. That was the acutest sense of his loss.

Matthew now was shaking with grief, head in hands, as Clare—and, less gently, Jerome—tried to comfort him.

Jerome accompanied Dr Jennings to Craig's study. Matthew and Clare remained in the kitchen. Matthew called Nicole. Their conversation was brief but it seemed to calm Matthew down.

Randall Jennings made tracks to leave. 'Your mum has had a whisky, guys, sit down with her and have the supper she's prepared. I need to get home but here's my number for each of you. Your mother has it too. Look after her and keep in touch. I'll take care of the death certificate. The people from the funeral parlour will be here in about an hour. Make sure you say your goodbyes before they arrive. I'll pop round tomorrow, Clare, with a prescription for a mild tranquillizer. For tonight, make sure one of your sons stays with you.'

'Matthew has a young wife now, Randall, remember?'

'So he does. I'd forgotten. Well, Jerome, make sure you stay over then.'

And he was gone.

A third place was laid at the table. It was eerie. They took their seats, Jerome handling the placing of the dishes on the table and the dishing up. Clare and Matthew were both shell-shocked. After supper, Jerome insisted that Matthew come through to the study with him to take leave of Craig. Again, this seemed so disconnected from recent reality, in which Craig was fully alive and engaged. Matthew reluctantly followed his brother.

'Go, darling, go. Would you like me to come with you?' Clare hesitantly offered.

'No, Mum, you stay here.' Jerome spoke authoritatively. 'You've been through quite enough in the last couple of hours. Make us all coffee if you can.'

And suddenly Clare was alone for the first time. Shaken, bereft, feeling weird. Will I always feel like this? she wondered, already trusting there would be a negative answer. But I'll need to get through this phase first, she realized, feeling sick to the pit of her stomach.

Within no time Jerome and Matthew were back. She had hardly put the kettle on. They made coffee together. Matthew actually looked more settled now.

'Can I invite Daniela and Luca over?' Jerome wanted to know.

'Maybe not yet, darling, maybe not yet. Let's wait till tomorrow to allow others into our private world, if you don't mind.'

'That's fine, Mum, I'll just go into the lounge and call her.' He took his mug of coffee and left Clare and Matthew to comfort each other, knowing they each had the best person in the other to do so.

Feeling strangely disembodied, Clare got into her empty bed knowing that this time Craig would not be joining her at a later stage. She felt disconnected from reality. Her beloved husband was lying cold in a funeral parlour. She was never to see him again. She shuddered. No new sobs now. She was drained and exhausted. After staring blankly at the walls for a couple of hours, she forced herself to read.

It so happened that she was in the process of rereading *To the Lighthouse*. She had always rather strongly identified with Mrs Ramsay, whose light and goodness drew others into her circle of warmth. She had never needed light and warmth more than now. She was always startled when she read Part 2, and now found herself wondering whether she would rather have predeceased Craig.

> *The hand dwindles in his hand; the voice bellows in his ear. Almost it would appear that it is useless in such confusion to ask the night those questions as to what, and why, and wherefore, which tempt the sleeper from his bed to seek an answer.*
>
> *[Mr Ramsay, stumbling along a passage one dark morning, stretched his arms out, but Mrs Ramsay having died rather suddenly the night before, his arms, though stretched out, remained empty.]*

It had always seemed brutal, this passage—never more so than now.

No, she wouldn't rather have predeceased Craig, but what happened next in her life? How was she to make that transition from a warm and happy marriage to the single life, the life of Grannie Mac, of Sister Bridget, of Father Sean? How was she to reconstruct herself as a single person?

How suddenly this has come, Lord. How unprepared I am. I shall not begin to ask why, Lord. Time enough for that later.

Despite the sense that a chasm lay at her feet, dangerously drawing her towards it, she felt thankful that she was still a mother, that she still had her two sons. Their lives, their women, their families, above all, they themselves would continue to give her life meaning and hope. She had to allow them into her pain. She had to be open to changing her role in their lives. She had to cease clinging because now it would *truly* make them claustrophobic. She needed simply to cling to the Rock which was Christ. Could she do it?

It was enormously comforting to know that Jerome was in his old room down the passage. She knew she could go to him for comfort, but she also knew he had his own memories and grief to deal with. He would have his breakfast with her in the morning.

Clare had helped others arrange funerals for their loved ones in the past. Sister Bridget and Nicole's mother Pam would assist her.

Jerome was staying with her until his uncle Duncan arrived from Vermont for the funeral. Duncan was coming not because he had been particularly close to Craig but to give Clare support. Clare appreciated this immensely, and would have loved having him to stay had the circumstances been different.

The day of the funeral approached. It was held on the Monday, to give Duncan a chance to arrive and recover from his trip over the weekend.

Jerome was pale and almost expressionless. Matthew was very tearful but trying to be strong for his mum. Daniela and Luca stood to one side, allowing Jerome to take the lead.

Father Sean delivered a short homily, commemorating Craig's good qualities of being hardworking, devoted to his wife (and sons), loyal, upright, unswerving, faithful to his calling as husband, father, businessman. The congregation in silence assented. Craig evoked admiration rather than warmth.

There was tea in the hall after the service. Clare felt herself carried by the love and support of her sons, first and foremost, and of her brother Duncan. And Nicole and Daniela were so sweet and affectionate, doing what they could in their quiet ways to support Clare and their men. Even Luca came over while Clare was surrounded by adults just to squeeze and kiss her hand, and say, 'I'm sorry, Auntie Clare.'

Randall Jennings was particularly attentive. His wife was in the same women's Bible study group as Clare and so they had a fair amount of contact, but it was Randall who had shared that unearthly moment with Clare, and who knew something of its impact. He had met her once or twice in the interim, to keep an eye on her and assess whether she needed more tranquillizers, or fewer, but so far he was impressed with her apparent calm acceptance of the situation, of how well she seemed to have adjusted to the reality of Craig's death. Both Randall Jennings and Clare knew, however, that one could rise to the occasion because of its momentous nature only to come crashing down after the major event of the funeral with all the warmth, contact, and even joy at being with long absent loved ones it necessarily brought in its wake.

Clare's aim had been to remain rooted and grounded in love, not to lose herself in the sorrows and joys of the moment but to keep a grip on the reality which was herself, her God, her sons. At some level she believed she was managing this, at another level she felt totally adrift, at sea. For almost three decades Craig had been her fortress. She no longer remembered life without him. Those few years between living under her parents' roof and marrying Craig were the tentative steps of a young woman growing in confidence as she blossomed into an adult.

She found it impossible to imagine her life as it would now become. And for the moment she tried not to try. She would immerse herself in the love of friends and relatives, try to be a support to Grannie Mac, and her sons, and let the future take its course when the time came.

Finally, Duncan was on his plane, back to the States. Jerome and Matthew and Clare sat around the kitchen table with their respective beverages, a cup of tea for Clare.

'What now?' Matthew asked.

'We need a lawyer to help us execute Dad's will,' Jerome said, matter-of-factly.

'It seems reasonably straightforward,' said Matthew. 'Most of everything goes to Mum, but you and I each receive half of a large investment.'

'All the same, Matthew, it would be irresponsible not to get a lawyer. We could ask Martin.'

'Fine, I just meant his will is not difficult to interpret.'

'We'll ask Martin, you two,' Clare intervened. 'He'll do it in an efficient and friendly way.'

'I'll call him now,' said Jerome.

They arranged to meet at Martin's office the very next afternoon. Both Clare and their sons would be financially secure even though certain investments had recently lost some of their value. They had always known Craig would make provision for them, but now that the time had come they realized the enormous debt of gratitude they owed him. Jerome especially was developing a new appreciation of the father he had struggled against for so many years. Periodically sharp stabs of regret flashed through him as he realized it was too late to make amends.

Spring

When the season of delight is over, who can say which of us
    will still be left in the land of the living?
Let us be merry while we may, for Spring is swift of foot
    and will not linger.
Listen to the song of the nightingale: Spring is coming.
In every thicket, Spring has quickened the fountain of joy.
The almond tree is decked with silvery blossom.
Be merry; be joyful; for Spring is fleet of foot,
    and will not linger.

(Ancient Oriental poem)

September

There is no Spring to me, Lord. Life seems dismal and grey. Despite the blossoms on the tree, there is only a yearning ache in my heart for the companion on my life's journey. My life seems bleak without him. Only you can bring me through this, Lord. I have never felt more helpless, more hopeless. Be my Rock, and my Redeemer. Lead me through this empty way that once again, eventually, I might experience your fullness. Guide me, blessed Lord. I am lost without Craig. I would be utterly lost without you.

C lare cast herself prostrate on her bed. The sobs were heaving themselves through her body, her mind and soul already drained from crying. She was overwhelmed, sometimes angry, sometimes scared, mostly just suffering from an overwhelming sense of loss and despair.

Sometimes she just stared into space, struggling to come to terms with the fact that her life partner was no longer there. What did anything matter? Even in her journal alternating blank and black pages were all she felt she could muster, and what would be the point of those?

At other times Clare sat on the grass, hugging her knees towards her. Her soul felt bruised and drained from crying. Would Craig ever come back? Would she ever see him again? These were not theological questions but instinctive cries. She needed him the way a child needs its mother. He'd been there for her for so long. Clare had always imagined their growing old together, enjoying their grandchildren, preferably at a ripe old age dying simultaneously in their sleep.

Craig's death was unscripted and brutal. *What were you thinking, Lord? Help me to understand.* She knew with an inward realization that she needed to trust and not interrogate, rest and not rebel, but every so often her outrage made itself felt. *Why?* was the overwhelming question that tore at her heart and mind. She had yet not found an answer.

Life had to continue. But how? Her world had suddenly stopped. And yet the planet was still hurtling through space at top speed.

She would invite Father Sean for tea. Maybe she would find his words and presence comforting at this time.

Indeed she did. He had so much experience helping people through their raw grief at the early stage after losing a loved one that nothing Clare felt or said could throw him. Instead, he could affirm the normalcy of her responses to her, and encourage her to believe her current state of mind would not be permanent.

'Father, what do you suggest I do to hurry on that next phase, when I will no longer be screaming in agony?'

'Be patient, dear Clare, be patient. One unfortunately has to live through each phase of the grieving process to get to the next stage. You can keep yourself busy, and surrounded by family and friends, but there *will* be times when you're alone and feeling desperate. These are the times when you need to trust things will improve, just hang in there with faith that they will improve, and indeed they will.'

'Thank you, Father, for your reassurance. I shall do my best to be patient and cling to my faith.'

'And maybe you can deepen your involvement with the parish as you will naturally find you have more time on your hands—time it may seem difficult to fill at first. We need a new coordinator for the catechism classes, more readers, more ministers of the Eucharist. But no pressure. When you surface there'll be time enough to attend to such possibilities. For now, focus on keeping yourself as sane and together as possible. It is not for nothing that there is a saying about "running mad with grief". Don't let that happen to you, dear Clare. Accept invitations when they come your way; don't be shy to depend on family and friends; and don't be afraid to call on me at any time. I am here for you, and so are your sons, other family and friends. You have a community of care surrounding you. Lean on us, dear Clare, and be assured of my special prayers for you at this time. Why don't you pop in at the parish office in a week's time and we can have another cup of tea together?'

'I'll do so, Father Sean. Thank you.'

He squeezed her hands reassuringly and with tear-filled eyes she saw him to his car.

Thank you for the comfort only you can bring, blessed Lord. Bless Father Sean and all those who are doing their best to comfort me. Help me to be mindful of the efforts they are making and to respond with grace and gratitude. Help me, dearest Lord, not to feel so utterly miserable. Help me to hold up my head again. Be my strength and my fortress.

For the first time in several weeks, Clare went into the house without a sense of total dread in the pit of her stomach. Could it be the beginning of the healing process?

October

I feel more at peace than previously, Lord, but life still seems a pale shade of grey. May the marriage of Jerome and Daniela infuse joy into my soul—or, if not directly into mine, then into theirs. Thank you that they have found each other.

But, dear Lord, do please enable me to experience joy again. Right now I seem numb with grief. Heal my soul, blessed Lord, and enable me, once again, to radiate your goodness to the world.

On her wedding day a couple of weeks later than originally planned, Daniela awoke to her favourite yellow bird making a racket outside her bedroom window. What a welcome to the world on this special day. She knew she and Jerome were taking the right step, and what was wonderful was that they all knew it was the right thing for Luca as well.

It was bittersweet though in the light of Jerome's father's recent death. And Daniela knew Jerome had only just begun to feel the consequences because it had taken her until recently to process the loss of her own father although he had died early in her childhood, which she believed was probably even more traumatic than what had happened to Jerome.

She tried to be supportive because she knew that Jerome felt things more deeply than he showed.

But today was her special day, hers and Jerome's, and she didn't want to dwell on what could make them both very sad. They had decided to go ahead with the wedding fairly soon to give everyone, herself and Luca included, as much of a sense of normality as possible.

Jerome himself would pick her up. One of Luca's teachers would give him a lift to the church to be in time for the small ceremony. Clare would be brought to church by Sister Bridget. Clare herself hadn't driven since Craig's death. She still felt too shaken and emotional to drive. Both Jerome and Daniela knew and liked Sister Bridget so they were happy to have her there, accompanying Clare. Matthew and Nicole were away on a delayed honeymoon.

The ceremony was short and sweet. The only tears were Clare's, and she tried to keep them unobtrusive. At least Craig had met and ultimately liked Daniela, she thought to herself, despite his initial reluctance and despite his reservations about their decision to get married. She needed to represent him now, and be strong for her sons and their wives. And for Luca, she smiled to herself. Here she at least felt she had a real role.

Along with Jerome's friend Martin, they all went out for a light lunch.

'I'd like to make a short speech,' Jerome said, almost unexpectedly. 'I'd like to start with my beautiful bride Daniela, and thank her for putting her trust in me. I will do my best to be worthy of that trust, Daniela. I do not want to disappoint you. With Luca being our first son, I hope we'll have more children to whom he'll be a great older brother. But no pressure on you, my love. I'm just sketching our long-term vision for these dear people to be aware of.'

Clare smiled. What a pleasure that it came naturally. She had barely smiled these last few weeks.

'And then, there's my mum. My speech would be incomplete without reference to her. Mum, we won't look back over the past few weeks. Instead, we want to invite you into our future. We are your family, and you are always welcome in our home, isn't she, Daniela?'

'Oh, of course, Jerome. Of course, dear Clare. We want you to be an integral part of our family, don't we, Luca?'

Again Clare smiled. Luca beamed from ear to ear. 'Yes, Auntie Clare, you are already one of my favourite people. When Jerome is too strict, or my mum in one of her strange moods, I will come and stay with you, in Jerome's old room. I love that space. I feel so at home there.'

Jerome was impressed by Luca's simple eloquence. But then there was so much about Luca which impressed him.

'Thank you, Jerome and Daniela. Thank you, Luca. It means a lot to me to be made so welcome in your lives. I don't take it for granted.'

Jerome continued to pay tribute to his father, even though it choked him up. Almost all of them were now close to tears. Sister Bridget and Martin remained strong for the four of them. Clare knew that the difficulties of Jerome's relationship with his father made the mourning process more painful rather than less. She admired his wanting to honour his father on this occasion. She looked down, as looking at Jerome would be too emotional.

When the formalities were all wound up, Jerome saw his mum and Sister Bridget to their car. Luca lingered with his mother. He felt confident that she would be happier now, and so would he, knowing she was cared for by Jerome. She would have to depend less on him, and for that he was grateful.

'Mum, Daniela and I would like to go away for a few days fairly soon. Would you . . . ?'

'Have Luca? I'd love to, darling. It'll cheer me up no end. And it will get me driving again. I'll have to give him lifts here and there, as well as some of his friends. Nothing like a teenager to make one rise to unreasonable demands. It will be a genuine pleasure. Tell Daniela and Luca they can depend on me. You just say when. Then I know when to start stocking up on his favourite foods.'

'Thanks, Mum, you're an angel, you really are. And remember we all three meant what we said—we want you to be an integral part of our family. In fact, you already are.'

'Thank you, darling, that means more to me than I can express, especially now, at this time. I need to forge a new identity, and you are helping me do it. Now get back to your dear wife and Luca. May you know every blessing.'

Jerome kissed his mother on her forehead and hugged her gently. 'We'll get in touch with our dates very soon, Mum. In the meantime, call or text me anytime you want to pop over or want one of us to come over to have a cup of tea with you.'

Clare got into the car, and squeezed Jerome's hand through the window. 'We'll keep in close contact, darling. Don't worry about me. Enjoy your new life.' And she was able to smile again. What an improvement that was. Craig would be proud of me, she found herself thinking. She turned to Sister Bridget with renewed energy and interest. Thank the Lord she had friends too.

Despite this happy interlude, life had changed irrevocably. Clare tried not to brood, but it was almost impossible not to. Time gaped before her like an enormous chasm. She and Craig had not spent that much time together engaged in active conversation during the morning and afternoon, but she had become accustomed to him being there, available, loving her, almost every hour of the day and night. The days when he went away on business trips by himself had almost ceased, and they had become more of a unified entity than ever before. The passion of youth had given way to a gentler, more harmonious and comfortable atmosphere between them, in which they each felt safe and valued. How would she feel safe and valued now?

Of course there were her sons but she dared not presume upon their love for her. They had other priorities now, and she did not want to make demands on them. She knew at some level that God was calling her to a deeper walk with him.

Would she accept that call, and respond to it? *Grant me the will and the strength and the courage, Lord*, she prayed. She knew the kind of solitude and soul-searching that would inevitably be required would not be easy, but then there were Sister Bridget and Father Sean, who would hold her hand and be alongside her as she took this next step on her journey. What would Craig have her do? This question would no doubt become a regular preoccupation of hers as she had noticed the question arise with other widows—seemingly not with Grannie Mac though. Perhaps she needed to get to know her mother-in-law better, especially now that they shared the profound loss of Craig. She could learn some independence from this strong woman, she believed.

Everything seemed more of an effort now. She suddenly felt an 'old fifty' rather than a 'young fifty'. Craig would hate me to capitulate, she found herself thinking. For my own sake he would want me to keep up my spirits. *Show me, Lord, how . . .*

Before long, Clare had an inspiration. She would speak to Elsa. The time for the Christmas party was drawing closer. She would make it even more special this year than usual. And with Elsa's help she would work out just how to do this. She had long since thought how great it would be to award a bursary or two to gifted students in need at this occasion. She and Craig had discussed the idea and she knew there was nothing better she could do in his memory. She could name the bursary after him. She would of course discuss the idea with Jerome and Matthew but she anticipated no objection from either of them.

She knew they would probably be only too relieved at a project which she could be enthusiastic about. Although they tried not to show it, she knew they were concerned about her low spirits, try as she might to hide them.

November

I cry less, Lord, but the days are still grey . . . When will this numbness pass? I am so grateful that Jerome and Daniela are settling down together and yet I had to make every effort not to cast sadness over the occasion. Restore me, Lord. Craig would not want me to disintegrate, surely, though he would understand my yearning, my brokenness, my longing for his voice, his touch, his stable presence in our home together. Can you grant me a sense of him again, dear Lord, that I might know his presence in some form once more? This gaping emptiness is killing me, Father, I need your healing touch. Be merciful to me, Lord. Let me feel Craig's loving touch.

Most mornings Clare woke and felt discouraged, demoralised, disjointed. It wasn't just Craig who was gone. That was bad enough, surely. Did she on top of this still have to feel out of sorts with herself? That calm centre from which she normally operated seemed all in a jumble, discordant, awry. Her prayers were voiceless, wordless, anguished cries for help, for succour, for strength, for peace. She had lost her peace—the greatest loss of all, for with it, all was bearable, without it, nothing was.

When would Craig return? she frequently found herself asking. It was an automatic response to an unfamiliar situation. He wouldn't. How many times would she still have to knock her head against this unwelcome reality? It was hard and cold and hateful. He would not return.

Clare's eyes were dry now. There were times when she simply had no tears left. And this was not a case of shaking off the blues of a temporary down mood—no, this was final, a new reality she needed to come to terms with. But how?

Sister Bridget's presence in her life at this time was very helpful, very comforting, most reassuring. Her generally cheerful disposition, her cheery voice, her hearty laugh, her sound advice and, above all, her shining example that life without a husband could be a happy one all coalesced into making Clare feel loved, almost hopeful, and somehow rebalanced.

Whenever Sister Bridget suggested staying over for the night, Clare gratefully accepted. Then they generally played scrabble at the kitchen table over a pot of tea.

These were the homely touches that made her feel her world was not so irrevocably shattered that some pieces could not be put back together again. And by the time Sister Bridget did actually leave, Clare was usually smiling.

She described the situation to Matthew when he popped in.

'That's excellent, Mum, really excellent.' And with a twinkle in his eye, he added, 'Just don't go running off to become a nun yourself! Jerome and I won't let you. If it's scrabble you're after, remember there's me and Nicole. We'd love to pit our skills against yours.'

'But I don't want to worry you, Matthew, you know I don't want to be a burden on you.'

'Mum, don't make me sad by talking like that. You know you can never be a burden to us. We love you infinitely and are committed to doing whatever it takes for you to be strong and happy again. Jerome and I are now the men in your life. Depend upon us as you once depended upon Dad.'

'I'll try, darling, I really will. In the meantime, though, you have Nicole and Daniela who depend on you, and as long as Sister Bridget and I are equal partners at scrabble and can share stories about parish life and other matters of no interest to you lot, I shall be grateful for her friendship.'

'Sure, Mum, as long as you don't feel she's all you have. We are very much there for you as well.'

'I know, darling, I hope you know I do. And thank you. Believe me, every night I thank God for you and Nicole, Jerome, Daniela and Luca and bless you all, and appreciate that you are all there for me. I count on you—I want you to know that.'

'That's as it should be, Mum. I'd better be on my way now, but we'll see you soon again. Nicole wants to cook you supper one of these days.'

'I look forward to it.'

Clare meditatively walked to her studio. She had hardly set foot in there these last few weeks. She would freshen it up, and look at the face of St Peter.

It was several hours later that she went back to the house. Almost imperceptibly, something within her heart and mind had shifted.

It was several weeks since Moira had been to sculpture classes, which was to be expected. At the funeral, where both she and her husband John were present, Moira had said she would call in a few weeks' time. Telephonically Clare and Moira had agreed to have a single class to wrap up the year. It naturally included a bit of catching up.

Was John transferred? Had he given up gambling? These were the questions on the tip of Clare's tongue but she restrained herself and let Moira lead the conversation. Soon enough it led to family decisions revolving around John. He'd managed to negotiate remaining in Cape Town but still being promoted. And the gambling? Clare stopped herself.

As though she had been asked, Moira continued, 'And as far as the gambling is concerned, Clare, Craig did a lasting good deed when he spoke to John. I'm not sure exactly what he said but I think it was something along the lines of how addiction could ruin a marriage and ruin a family. I think Craig must have pleaded with him on behalf of our children, something I was way too angry to do myself. So as a couple, and as a family, we are deeply indebted to your husband. Oh, Clare . . .' Moira reached out her hands as Clare's eyes filled with tears. 'Forgive me for talking so freely . . . It is all still so fresh. It was insensitive of me.'

'Not at all, dear Moira,' Clare smiled through her tears. 'I only wish Craig could know what a positive impact he had.'

'Maybe he did, Clare, maybe he could sense that he was making a profound and lasting impact on John. Men sometimes know these things.'

'Yes, you're right.' Clare heaved a sigh. 'Perhaps he did.'

They did some work on the bust of Moira's elder son which she was busy sculpting, and discussed whether Moira should take it home to work on over Christmas, but decided against it.

'I need you to be with me, Clare, when I work on it, and I enjoy it all so much more when you are. Besides, we're bound to have a busy time with the house full of kids, and I'm trying to keep this as a surprise for the family, most especially for my son. So all things considered, it makes sense to keep it safe here in your studio, and I'll contact you as soon as the kids are back at school to arrange for our first class, that is, if you think you'll be ready.'

'I'll make sure I'm ready, Moira. I look forward to it.'

The two women embraced and parted. With tears in her eyes, Clare closed up the studio, went inside to her bedroom, lay on her bed and wept. *Does it get any easier, Lord?* she asked, already knowing the answer, but needing immediate consolation nonetheless. *Help me, Lord, to trust you, that you will bring me through this pain. They say crying is part of the healing process, but Lord, every time I think I've reached the next stage of grieving, as they describe it, so often do I seem to slip right back. Draw me on and out, dear Lord. Bring me through this as swiftly as possible. I do not like feeling helpless.*

Sister Bridget had insisted that Clare call her anytime of the day or night if she was feeling particularly low. Now was such a time. Sister Bridget undertook to pop round straight after supper and the two friends sat companionably in the lounge, knitting, talking, and dipping into the news every now and then. She left at about nine, by which stage Clare was feeling more herself again.

She still cried herself to sleep that night, but her tears were gentler, more peaceful than earlier. *I know I'll come through this, Lord. Thank you for friends, thank you for my children. Bless us all with your sweet love, gentle Lord.*

Clare felt distinctly brighter when she woke up the next morning.

Clare picked up the phone to call her mother-in-law and then swiftly put it down again. Feeling rather ashamed, she picked it up again, more deliberately this time, to invite her to tea at Rhodes Memorial. She must be hurting as badly as I am, Clare reflected, possibly even more so. I still have my sons. She has neither husband nor son. She has only me and Jerome and Matthew. We need to be there for her. Beginning now.

'Hello, Mother,' Clare tried to speak in her brightest tone. 'How are you?'

'I'm bearing up, dear, thank you. I've been thinking a lot of what you must be going through. Craig's passing has brought back so many memories of George's death.'

'Let's talk about it when we're together, Mother. I'd like to take you out to tea. What time can I pick you up?'

Before long they were seated in the shade at the Rhodes Memorial restaurant. The grand setting seemed the perfect backdrop for Clare's rather majestic mother-in-law. Grannie Mac looked stronger than Clare had expected.

'How are you, Mother?' Clare asked again, this time able to make eye contact, and leaning forward gently.

'Strangely enough, I'm not doing too badly, Clare, dear. My biggest concern is for you; also for Matthew, who I know was very close to Craig. You know, Clare, the difference between you and me is that I will probably see Craig first, sooner than you. Quite a thought that is.'

'Oh, Mother, that does seem to be a strange way of looking at things. Please do not hasten the day!'

'Thank you, dear, I won't. But I want you to have the greatest peace and comfort possible in the situation you now find yourself. Have Jerome and Matthew been supportive?'

'You know, Mother, they both have in their different ways, but both of them really have their hands full—Jerome with his new family, his studies, his karate classes, and Matthew with his delicate bride. I do not want to be a burden to them . . .'

'You won't be, Clare, trust me. You are too gentle and sweet ever to be a burden—unlike me with my imperious ways!'

Oh, so she knows, does she? Clare wondered to herself. Aloud she said, 'Of course not, Mother, we love having you around. And remember now that Craig's gone,' it still seemed strange saying that, thinking it and, above all, feeling it, 'you need to depend more completely on us, the three of us you have left.'

'Oh, I shall, Clare, dear, but then you in turn must promise to tell me to stop *before* you get heartily sick of me, and not afterwards. Just as you don't want to be a burden to your boys, so do I not want to be a burden to any of you. I'd sooner die.'

'Please, Mother, don't speak of dying like that. It is not for us to choose the day nor the hour. That is up to the Lord. It is simply for us to do our best each day and trust him to provide for all our needs, and I have a strong feeling that for the foreseeable future our needs will be supplied by one another. We should embrace this and do nothing to prevent it. I suspect it's God's perfect plan for us.'

'When you put it like that, Clare, I cannot but agree. Remember that I'm getting on in years though. It's not that I'm trying to be morbid. But in the meantime I shall accept the new state of things if you want me to with gratitude.'

'Thank you, Mother, yes, I do. So let's agree to be fully cooperative with each other and with the boys, and I'm sure Craig would be very proud of us all!'

They went for a gentle stroll after tea, and when Clare dropped Grannie Mac off, they were more bonded than ever.

Bless her, Lord, may she not be her own worst enemy. And yet let me not disparage her thoughts regarding her own death. She is in her eighties after all. Thank you that she seems willing to accept our love and help. And I know, Lord, you'll give Jerome and Matthew the love and grace and patience they will need.

Once home, it seemed rather strange but Clare decided to have a sherry. She watched international news as she did so. Her thoughts turned to Vermont.

The following week Clare found she was still catching her breath, but acute grief was beginning to make way for resignation. It had been an eventful year. At the beginning of it, Clare had had her husband and her two sons close to her. Nicole was in hospital and, to everyone's joy and relief, her healing had been transformative. For that, and for the marriage of Matthew and Nicole, Clare was eternally grateful. Daniela and Luca had also enriched all their lives, and Clare was deeply content that her elder son too was happily hitched.

But oh, the loss of her husband! How would she ever get over it? Or should she simply accept that she never would?

Clare decided she would accept Duncan's invitation to go and spend Christmas with his family in Vermont. She would leave the young couples to enjoy their first Christmas, alone, together, in whichever way they chose, without having to worry about her in any way. There would surely be future Christmases together. This time she would pack her grief in a suitcase along with her winter clothes and do her best to be a blessing to Duncan, Sheila, and their children.

She stood up from the bench next to the goldfish pond and walked resolutely indoors, to the computer from where she would do her first booking herself in many years.

Tears pricked her eyes but she believed she was doing the right thing. Grief and peace mingled together and formed her new reality. She would be brave and look forward. She had to believe that the time would come when it would be possible for her to be happy again.

During the course of the next couple of weeks, Clare went shopping for Christmas presents with Elsa, and Pam kindly offered to help organize the party with Elsa during Clare's absence.

Jerome and his lawyer friend Martin helped her put the Craig MacMillan bursary fund in place. Both Jerome and Matthew were thrilled with her plan to commemorate their father in this way.

Clare also arranged for an outing for Grannie Mac on Christmas Day with members of her Presbyterian Church congregation. Grannie Mac was touched, and happy that Clare was taking the positive step of travelling abroad for a change of scene while still spending Christmas with loved ones.

'The first Christmas, the first Easter, the first birthday apart—these are all particularly painful moments, dear. I am glad you are dealing with Christmas in a resourceful way.'

Jerome and Matthew would take turns popping in at the house to make sure everything was fine, and to open up windows for fresh air. They each still had a set of keys. Naturally they would also feed the goldfish.

Summer again

I shall always keep a green bough in my heart.
    A singing bird will come.

                                                  (Chinese proverb)

The day before her departure Matthew called.

'Mum, have you already arranged transport to the airport, or can Nicole and I take you?'

'I would love to be seen off by you two gentle people,' Clare replied.

'Good. Then let us know what time you need to check in, and we'll make sure we have time for a coffee beforehand.'

'I look forward to it. There could be no nicer way for me to set off to Vermont than exactly as you describe it.'

The day approached. Clare was ready but her heart was heavy. It was so different doing things without Craig's support. She had her children's support—she knew that—but it was different from being the sole apple of her husband's eye. He was exclusively devoted to her, and his every breath had her wellbeing as goal. His breath flowed no longer. Nevertheless, she put on a brave face and greeted Matthew with a warm smile and a hug, enlisting his help for her medium-sized bag filled with winter clothes and Christmas gifts for the family. Matthew gallantly opened the door for his mother, who sat behind him so that she could talk to Nicole.

Nicole looked pale but quietly radiant, as was her wont. They conversed lightly and brightly, Matthew concentrating on the driving but glowing as his two favourite women shared ideas. Of course, Nicole's health was of paramount importance.

'It's going well, Auntie Clare,' she said. She had obtained permission to take her time to call Clare something like 'Mum' but yet different from what she called her own mother. She had not yet come up with a suitable term. 'At the airport we are going to share something with you that we hope will make you happy.'

'Oh, you two mystery people! I am happy even at the prospect of your news. And nothing can please me more than good news regarding your health, Nicole, you know that.'

'I know, Auntie Clare, and I so appreciate the support you have been throughout my illness and also during these first few months of our marriage. Knowing you were there rooting for me gave me such security and strength.'

Before long they were ordering drinks from the quietest café they could find at Cape Town International.

'Mum, we have something urgent and very confidential to tell you.' Matthew's voice and facial expression convinced her it was something good. 'Nicole's pregnant.'

'What?! Oh, my Lord, this is beyond my wildest imaginings . . . So soon, and all healthy? You two take my breath away. What a wonderful way to start your married life together. You are blessed, and will be the most marvellous blessing to your children. Am I to be a grandmother? I'm over the moon! Congratulations. Nicole, let me hug you. And you too, darling Matthew. You are both about to experience a new dimension in your lives, one that will deepen and enrich you beyond description. Oh, let me be quiet, and tell me more . . . I'm out of breath with excitement.'

Clare paused for breath and to let the enormity of their news sink in.

'Auntie Clare, we have told only my parents, and now you. Not even my sister Lucy nor Jerome and Daniela are going to be told at this stage. My health as you can imagine is too delicate for us to be over-confident. We want to take my pregnancy very gently and give our baby all the chance in the world to develop with maximum privacy.'

'You are right, my angels, quite right. You can trust me fully. Neither my brother nor sister-in-law nor your cousins, Matthew, will hear a word of this. But oh, they'll find me glowing with a joy they'll find hard to explain. And I will be praying for you two, and your baby now, with more zeal than ever. Nicole, are you still seeing your haemotologist from time to time? Does he know? And do you have a good gynaecologist?'

'I'm sorted, Auntie Clare, don't worry about me. My mum and Matthew have made sure I'm in safe hands. My haemotologist is delighted at this bold step we've taken and he says all the hormones and other changes generated by a pregnancy can only do me good. The occasional bout of nausea I have is like nothing compared to what I experienced during treatment, and both doctors and my mum assure me it will soon pass. They are right, aren't they?'

'Yes, of course they are. After three months you'll forget you ever were nauseous. Sorry you have to be reminded of your treatment but thank God it's over. Oh, you two have so blessed me. I have not known such joy since Dad died, Matthew. How happy and proud he would have been . . .'

'You represent him now, Mum. Know that. And he would be so proud of you holding the fort. Remember we depend on you. Your prayers sustain us. Your example encourages us to be brave like you. And we want you to be one hundred per cent involved in our baby's life. You will be such a blessing to him or her. We know you will.'

'Thank you both. And thank you for sharing this precious moment of your lives with me. I feel transformed. I guess I need to think about catching that plane now but with what a different spirit from the one I woke up to this morning. Through you the Lord has put a new song in my heart, and I shall carry it with me to the end of my days.'

'Which will mercifully be a long way off, Mum,' Matthew reminded her. 'Just because Dad has left us doesn't mean you have to follow in his footsteps. We want your involvement, we want your presence in our lives,' and they all embraced, with the unborn child securely at the centre of their being.

Clare boarded that plane with a spring in her step. She had everything to look forward to. She had the best sons and the best daughters-in-law imaginable, and she had a future. She would cease brooding and instead embrace her new life with faith in the goodness of God, and in his special provision for her. She would trust him to continue enabling her to be a blessing to her loved ones, sensitive to their needs and lending a helping hand where required. Only loving memories of Craig would accompany her.

She would move into the future with joy.

Acknowledgements

My thanks go to

Anne Schuster, my Ideal Reader, for being Seriously Impressed and Totally Awestruck at just the right moments during the writing process.

Gwenaëlle Fossard, from Les Héritiers Matisse, for her kind cooperation and gracious permission to use the cover image of Henri Matisse's *Goldfish*.

Shirley Wittridge, the novel's first reader, for her incisive comments.

Carla Joy van Zyl, for providing me with a youthful perspective.

Lisa Fisher, for careful feedback and encouragement.

Dr Mike du Toit, clinical haematologist, for generously providing invaluable medical insights.

Felice Marano, for assisting me with the Italian connection and for happy times in Naples and Capua.

Kashiya Mbinjama, for her insightful responses.

My elder son David Sipho, whose alternative take on life challenges existing norms, which stretches my boundaries.

My younger son Mark Thabo, for inspiring me with his gentleness and Christian faith.

Finally, my husband, Roy du Pré, for his love and support along the way.

Lightning Source UK Ltd.
Milton Keynes UK
UKOW01f0436130616

276070UK00001B/32/P